PUFFI

The Earth Giant

Melvin Burgess was born in 1954 and was brought up in Sussex and Berkshire. After leaving school he moved to Bristol, where he was generally unemployed, with occasional jobs, mainly in the building industry. He wrote, on and off, unsuccessfully. He moved to London in 1983, where he met his partner, dancer Avis von Herder, and began a small business marbling fabrics for the fashion industry. His first book, *The Cry of the Wolf*, was published in 1990.

Melvin Burgess now writes full time and lives in Lancashire with his partner Avis and their young children, Oliver and Pearl.

B285

Chapter 1

Peter was woken in the night by a terrible bang. The whole house shook as if a giant were beating at it with the flat of his hand. Peter sat up in bed holding his breath. He expected to see the wall shudder and break open. Then he heard the bawling and shrieking and he knew it was just the wind . . . but such a wind! It shook the house as if the air was really a solid thing.

He ran to the window. There was no rain or clouds. He could see the dusty moon and strange stars shining dully. The sky was full of shapes. The air was hot and dry. His throat and nose were dried up.

There was a shriek next door from his mother as something boomed and banged against the walls. Suddenly, Peter stopped being frightened. He grinned with excitement; this was different! He ran next door. His parents were sitting up in bed in the small light of the bedside lamp. His father was staring up at the ceiling.

'It'll have the roof off,' he exclaimed. The ceiling creaked. Peter stared up – could the wind really do that?

His mother moaned as something crashed and shattered outside. 'There goes another tile,' she said. She rolled her eyes and pursed her lips as if the whole thing was typical, absolutely typical. She let out another small shriek as something banged on the door downstairs – a bit of wood or something rolling about.

'Now it wants to come in!' she said, and she giggled. Peter shouted gleefully. She scowled at him. He was so noisy! 'Go next door and see if Amy's all right, will you, darling? She can come in with us if she's scared.'

Peter pulled a face . . . not because he didn't want to go and see his little sister – she was seven – but because he was never allowed to come and sleep with his mother, no matter how bad his dreams were.

Amy was sitting on the window ledge. She almost jumped out of her skin when he opened the door, as if she thought the storm had come into her room in person. Peter pulled a silly face at her and her hands flew up to her mouth and she giggled delightedly. She adored her big brother.

She ran and grabbed him. 'Look, Peter, look,' she ordered. Peter ran with her to the window and looked out.

The garden was being destroyed. Plants were ripped out of the ground, bushes and shrubs blown flat. The fences were wagging and flapping in the earth. Things that belonged to the ground had taken to the air. Cardboard boxes, bits of wood, twigs and even small branches the wind had torn from the trees were flying like crazy bats in and out of the light from the house. The dustbin was crashing

2

about between the fence and the house. It kept banging into the walls. What would happen if it hit a window?

'What do you think they want?' demanded Amy seriously. Peter stared at her in a little fright. She said such strange things. Then he grinned. He saw what she meant. All the ordinary objects of the day had come to life in this strange night. They were flying through the air in panic.

The really wonderful thing was the tree at the bottom of the garden. It was a tall fir tree, straight as a soldier pointing at the sky. It used to tower above the houses. Now it was shaped like a hoop. The wind was bending it so low that its tip was ripping the top off the privet hedge around the garden, but it refused to snap. It lashed backwards and forwards, sending small bushes and sticks and bits of rubbish flying.

Peter was delighted. 'It could cut you in half!' he yelled. 'It could send you flying through the air.' He was thinking of those cartoons where people get flung miles by bent trees. But this didn't look like a cartoon; even from here he could see how deadly the tree was. 'If it hits the dustbin it'll knock it for miles,' he cried. He'd give anything to see the dustbin knocked like a cricket ball by the lashing tree. The bin bounced high on the wall and went sailing down the lawn, but it wasn't getting near the tall tree.

Outside, somewhere in the darkness, was a terrible banging noise, almost an explosion. Amy squealed and hid behind her brother.

'What was it?' she begged. Peter shook his head anxiously. There was a cry from next door.

'Amy . . .' It was their mother, anxious for her baby. 'Are you all right, darling? Come in with us . . .'

Peter watched her jealously. 'Come into my bed,' he whispered. But Amy shook her head. She climbed back onto the window-sill.

Peter was so delighted she was staying with him he began clowning around, jumping up and falling down. Amy watched him, giggling. Then she turned round and watched the tree outside again.

'I'm going out!' announced Peter suddenly.

'Don't be silly,' said Amy scornfully.

'You're coming too!' Peter seized her hand and pulled. Amy screeched in fright and pulled back.

'Peter!' yelled his father from next door.

Peter carried on pulling but he put his finger to his lips. 'Ssssh . . .' Obediently, Amy carried on pulling away, but in silence.

'Come with me!' he dared, knowing she never would.

Outside in the darkness, something groaned like a man. It was huge and terrible. What throat could make such a sound! Peter cringed back from the window. Amy jumped for her bed and he ran to be near her. Something was in terrible pain. It went on for so long! He could feel the hair bristling on his neck. He longed for it to be over. It wasn't fair that anything should suffer like that however big

4

and awful it was.

There was a wrenching noise, a tearing, splitting sound. The groaning began to pulse. Then, a crash.

Silence. Even the wind was still.

Peter stared at his sister. He was kneeling by her bed holding the covers. Gradually the wind outside returned to life.

'What was it?' he whispered.

Amy looked calmly at him. 'The trees are falling down,' she said.

'Are they?' It must be right; that groaning had been the wood splitting and straining. He was impressed that Amy had known. She seemed less frightened than he was. She stared at him, as if the whole storm had suddenly stopped interesting her.

There was only the beating of the wind, the thrashing leaves, the objects in the air banging into each other. Amy lay down in her bed. Peter licked his dry lips and glanced at the window. That noise had been awful. It had shaken him but she was so calm.

'It was a giant,' he said. 'A giant coming to get you . . .'

Amy turned to look at him. 'It was the big old tree on the river. Next to Barrow Hill. That's what it was,' she said, almost to herself. She nodded. 'That's what it was . . .'

'That's miles away!'

Amy turned away to face the wall and lie down. 'Go to bed, Peter,' she said, as if she was the big one and he her little brother. Peter stared angrily at her.

His father called from next door. 'Peter . . . back to bed!'

Peter groaned. He'd never be able to sleep through this, it was stupid. But his father insisted. He always made him do the right thing, even when it was such a waste of time . . . like sleeping when the world was being blown to bits!

His father yelled. Peter trailed miserably back to bed.

Alone, Amy lay very still and wondered why the air was so terrible. Tonight there were things in her head she was certain she had never thought. She wondered how she would find the world when she went out the next day . . . all blown about with familiar things and hidden things all mixed up and scattered over the fields and streets. She wondered why the ancient tree by the river had blown down and what it meant. Tomorrow she would go and see.

She wondered what secrets were being torn out of the earth by the angry air.

'No school today,' bawled Mrs Lee. Peter howled in pleasure. It was morning. It had gone on for hours! There were still no clouds and the air was so dry it chapped your lips. The sky had changed. It was dirty and brown and red and yellow and the sun shone through a haze of dry mists.

The Lee family always firmly behaved as if everything was normal. Everyone had got up and got

6

ready as if they could really leave the house and go out. Standing by the window, Peter and Amy could see objects that belonged to the ground still flying about as if they were made out of paper. Once, they saw a bird blown past. They couldn't tell if it was alive or dead. The wind was deafening even with the door closed.

'I want to go out,' said Amy. Peter looked at her in surprise. She didn't seem to be teasing.

'You'd get killed,' yelled her dad. He opened the back door just a crack. The air rushed into the kitchen and blew the cornflakes to the ground. The paper on the notice board flapped violently and all around, letters, newspapers and other bits of paper took to the air.

'Shut it, shut it,' Mrs Lee yelled. 'You're not going to work this morning!' she exclaimed. Behind her head, past the kitchen window, an enormous blue tarpaulin suddenly appeared and began a crazy dance outside the window. It didn't blow away, it just danced there. It looked as if it was trying to tell them it wanted to come in.

'Go away!' commanded Mrs Lee. The tarpaulin flapped desperately at her and vanished.

'Well, I should try . . .'

'You can't drive in this. All it needs is a branch or something to break the windscreen . . . the trees are going over everywhere.'

Mr Lee looked doubtfully out of the window. Going outside had never been dangerous before. It was difficult to believe it was now.

7

'It's great ... it's absolutely flattening every-thing!' said Peter. He begged Amy to come and see out the front but she was watching her father. Mr Lee was ready for work. He hovered by the back door with his briefcase. He listened to the wind howling. He opened the door again, just a crack. The wind rushed eagerly around the room.

'I'm making a run for it!' he yelled suddenly.

'No ...' cried Mrs Lee. But he put his arm round her, kissed her and dashed suddenly out of the door.

'Idiot!' yelled his wife. She rushed to the door after him but she wouldn't go out. Amy and Peter ran upstairs so they could watch him from the window.

Mr Lee had to force his way through the wind. He had to fight the door to the garden at the back for nearly a minute before it agreed to open and let him squeeze through. He gazed nervously at the garage door and then pushed his way through the wall of air to the top of the short drive where he could see up and down the road. He stared for a moment. Then he ran back, blown like a piece of paper down the drive and into the house.

Peter and Amy ran down to meet him.

'David at number three and another car – the big red Volvo further down – they've both been crushed by trees. The road's blocked!' He opened his coat. 'There're trees flat on the ground all over ... like skittles. Day off,' he sighed. He hated missing work. 'Courtesy of the weather!'

'Then the weather's got more sense than you

have,' grumbled his wife. She was relieved. She put her arms round him and kissed his cheek. 'Idiot,' she said fondly.

All day Peter was beside himself with excitement and wanted to play loud, wild games with his sister, but Amy wasn't interested. She was so quiet she worried her mother, who kept putting her hand on her forehead and wondering if she was ill. She needed to stay still to listen to the strange messages that moved in her mind like quick lizards. She didn't know yet what was waiting for her in the meadow by the fallen tree, but she knew she couldn't go there with anyone, not even with Peter. It was for her alone.

The storm passed at midday. Peter and Amy were watching TV when they noticed how quiet it was. They turned almost together to look at the window. A piece of cardboard fell out of the air. They ran to look.

Outside, all the things that had come to life were settling. Twigs, leaves, scraps of paper and other rubbish were falling out of the sky. Above them the sun like a dizzy red eye stared down.

'Now we can go out,' cried Peter. They ran to the kitchen to get their coats, but once they had them on they stood nervously by the door. They were scared of outside now. This wind was not like other winds; it might come back as suddenly as it had vanished. If you were out there when it came back . . .

In the end their parents made them have their lunch first, and they weren't sorry. But the wind stayed light and the weather forecast claimed the hurricane had gone away for good. Mr and Mrs Lee kept looking nervously outside at the scattered roof tiles and uprooted trees. But the weather was getting better all the time and in the end Peter's nagging wore them down. The two children were wrapped up, even though it was warm outside, and sent out of the front door with orders not to go far.

'And stay with Peter!' their mother ordered Amy as they walked up the drive.

The town was quiet. All the roads were blocked, the cars still. It was another world. Peter wasn't interested in the meadows. It was much more interesting to walk the streets and see the damage done to the town. Amy walked quietly beside him and waited while he chattered and explored.

There were fallen trees on every street. There seemed to be many more of them than when they stood tall, as if they had blown in from all around. They lay on top of cars that peered out from between the leaves, their bonnets and roofs crushed like tins by the fallen trunk. One had fallen onto a house. It leaned heavily against the front. Its branches had smashed the windows and gone inside. They could see the green sprays of leaves pushing a lampshade aside.

Peter rushed to and fro, kicking the heaps of green leaves the wind had stripped from the branches, chucking sticks at the bits of rubbish that had fallen on telephone wires and hedge tops, climbing the tangled branches of the fallen trees. He tried to get his sister to climb with him in the branches of a sycamore that lay flat across the road a few hundred yards from their house. Amy smiled and shook her head.

'Baby!' yelled Peter angrily. Amy was no fun, today of all days when there was so much fun to be had. Normally she did whatever he wanted. He climbed high into the thickness of the leaves and began shaking the tree violently and hooting like a gorilla. Amy watched the swaying branches closely. Peter was out of sight. She glanced up and down the road nervously, then crept quickly round the corner. When she was out of sight, she ran for the meadows.

Her mother had told her to stay with Peter but this was more important. Amy climbed a fence and hurried across the grass towards the river. She often spent hours wandering here. It was her land. There were no roads. The river was deep in places but never fast as it rolled this way and that among the cows and pastures. She knew exactly which way to go.

As she hurried along, Amy looked at the damage the great wind had done. It had flattened the wheat and barley. There were huge holes punched into the fields on the hillsides, as if a giant had walked that way and left his footprints behind him. Up on

11

Barrow Hill which she could see from far away with so many trees down, all the grass was flat and the trees and bushes had all been stripped away. Closer by the birds flitted nervously about the branches of fallen trees. They were lost, their world of trees lying on the ground. Two big black crows jumped nervously when Amy came out suddenly from behind a hedge. They cawed and flew up into a willow tree still standing near a backwater. They were feeding on a sheep killed in the storm.

Soon the willows along the banks gave way to a small woodland that grew right up to the water's edge. The old oak that Amy wanted to see stood hidden among the young trees like a stranger. It was more ancient than anything she knew. It had split in so many places it was not much more than a shell. You could sit inside it. There were only a few stubby, broken branches left but on the ground were the remains of the huge arms that once spread far around it. Below it in the bank, the river had washed away the earth and exposed a net of roots.

As she got close, Amy began to dawdle. 'It won't be down,' she scoffed at herself. She stood still and began to pull the leaves off a bush. Then she sighed. Although she shouldn't know, although there was no way of her knowing, she was perfectly certain that the tree was down after all. She ran forward.

The tree had fallen forward into the water pulling up a vast disc of earth behind it, a mass of soil and great stones and snapped roots and clay. The tree had been broken down by the wind and weather and old age, but the roots had continued to grow, hidden away out of sight. They were far bigger than what showed above the ground, like another tree that had been hidden underground all the time. There was a huge crater in the river bank behind it where the tree had once stood.

Amy stood nervously at the edge of the pit for a minute. Then she sat down on the grass at the edge of the crater and slid down on her bottom over the broken damp soil and rubble and clay . . . down into the earth.

It was cold . . . the cold of the underground, where there had been no sun ever. It smelt dead. She began to scrape away at the earth. Her hands were no good, she found a stone with a broad edge. She scraped carefully at first, nervous in case she hit something and damaged it. When nothing appeared where she expected it she scraped harder, deep into the ground. But there was nothing there.

She moved to another spot and began again but she uncovered only stones and roots. She tried again and again. All her senses told her there was something here, but the clay was completely dead.

At last she gave up and sat unhappily in the crater. She felt like crying. It was all wrong!

Then, slowly into her mind came a cold, vast presence: the huge ball of clay and roots the tree had torn from the ground. She turned her head to look up at it. It towered above her into the sky. It was difficult to think such a huge object had been underground all the time; it seemed somehow vaster

13

than the ground. And then Amy realised. What she was looking for – what had called her – wasn't underground any more. It was where it had always been – held in the embrace of the roots of the old oak. Only now it was high up over her head . . .

Amy scrambled up out of the hole and began to toil up the cliff face of roots, clay and stones. She wasn't good at climbing but she was confident now. She knew where to go. She found a great broken root sticking out and sat on that, and she began to scrape.

The clay fell away in sticky clumps at first, but after the first layer it got harder. The earth and stones were packed so tightly together. She would have liked to dig with a stick, but she didn't dare. She might hurt something. Then she began to panic that Peter might come back and see and she began to shovel with both her hands as fast as she could, breaking her nails and tearing her skin. At last, she found what she was looking for.

It was almost the same colour as the earth, a deep reddish colour. It was smooth and shiny and only slightly warmer than the earth. Amy brushed it with her hand. It was round and firm. No one else would have recognised it, but Amy knew. It was part of an arm.

She moved a little further up the cliff of broken roots and began again. She dug the clay and stones away in handfuls, revealing the skin closer towards the neck. There was a pattern on it, where gravel and little stones had pressed into it over the years.

14

A few more handfuls and the neck and the strong curve towards the shoulder came into view. Then, pressed firmly in the earth, the edge of an ear.

Amy stared. It had been a dream but it was real. She touched the skin on the ear gently with her finger. The skin was cold but Amy also knew it was not dead. It was the cold of someone, a woman or girl, who had been asleep for a long, long time – since before the old oak tree was an acorn. She had been asleep for hundreds or thousands of years, and now she was awakening again.

There was no movement; the sleeper lay as still as the stones around her. Amy slowly stroked her neck and began to imagine it was getting warmer. It was only the heat of her own hand. Now she began to realise that everything was so big – the shoulder so long and high, the arm so broad. She was almost twice as big as a grown-up. It was a giant in the earth.

Trembling, Amy climbed down from her perch and stood at the bottom staring up. The skin had been dyed the colour of the earth over the years, you could hardly see it from down there. How had she known... why had she come? The woman had been born in the storm, now she was coming to life. All that wind, all those broken windows and roofs, all those flattened cars and fallen trees... all of it had been only to pull the sleeping woman out of the ground.

Amy brushed the earth from her clothes.

'Soon you can come out,' she said anxiously. She sat down as if to wait, but then she heard Peter calling her and stood up. He was running towards her across the field.

Peter was furious with Amy for leaving him like that. Suddenly she didn't seem to need him at all. But all his anger was forgotten at the sight of the ruined tree.

He drew up to her and stood there gasping for breath and staring down into the cold-smelling pit. He looked oddly at her. 'How did you know?' he panted.

Amy looked away and shrugged. 'I just did.'

Peter pulled a face. He didn't like to be proved wrong by his little sister. He couldn't understand how it had blown down because there was so little for the wind to grab hold of.

'The water washed the earth away from under it and made it fall,' he explained. Amy said nothing. She stood and watched the tiny little leaves, still alive, flickering in the water.

Peter jumped down into the crater to explore. He dug at the earth, pulled at stones. Amy winced. She stared, tense in every muscle.

'It was hundreds of years old!' said Peter at last. He was angry. The tree had been special. All the other fallen trees had been fun but this was different. How unfair that something so old and grand should be dying at their feet.

He didn't want to stay by the dying tree.

'I know – let's go and have a look at the plan-

16

tation. I bet those little trees are lying down like matchsticks!'

Amy glanced nervously up at the roots. She had done what she had to. Now, for a time, she was free.

'Yes – come on!'

She ran excitedly after her brother to see the new wonder.

Chapter 2

Amy was scared of what the giant would be like when she came out, but she was terribly anxious that she should come out safely. There was danger. Other people might find her and try to take her away. Dogs might find her. All Amy wanted to do was wait by the old tree and watch her emerging but she couldn't go there as often as she wanted, because she might make Peter curious. He always wanted to know what she was doing. Amy would have loved to share the secret with him, but she knew that was impossible . . . just as she knew that the old tree had fallen in the gale, just as she knew there was someone waiting there, hidden in the roots.

As it was she went every other evening and he was still wondering.

'Have you got a friend down there?' he demanded. Amy said nothing. Peter was angry that she seemed to have forgotten him.

Gradually, the long woman began to emerge from her prison of mud. The earth washed away around the muscles of her back down to her leg, her ear, the clotted mass of thick black hair, crushed into the earth. Amy longed to see her face but it was turned away as if she was staring into the clay.

Amy had been scared to dig because she felt it was wrong to help, in the same way it was wrong to help a butterfly come from its chrysalis. She might hurt something. But as the days passed and the woman was still there, unmoving, part of the earth itself, Amy became afraid that she might never break away. She began carefully to brush the sand softly away from the face. Soon the head stuck like a stone out of the clay, and Amy was able to lay her fingers gently on her friend's cheek.

She knew that she would never desert the giant, whom she loved.

'Won't you wake up soon?' she begged.

Under Amy's fingers there was a brief flicker, like a mouse squirming. Amy screamed. She fell, tumbling past the roots and earth into the crater. When she stood up she was frightened she would see the eye staring down at her. But the head stared blindly into the clay, like an unfinished statue. Amy brushed herself down – she was always getting into trouble for coming home with her clothes in a mess these days – and climbed out of the hole. Then she began to run away across the fields, back home. The woman was coming alive at last.

It was a kind of birth. In bed that night Amy couldn't sleep because she knew that she ought to be out there in the dark by the river keeping watch. But she didn't dare. It was so dark in the meadows. It was half a mile on her own and when she got there, what would she find? So she raged at herself and lay between the warm covers and did nothing while the woman struggled alone.

She meant to stay awake all night so that she could be up as soon as the light cleared the sky. But the long hours went by so slowly, and she fell asleep. When she woke up the sun was already high.

Amy leapt out of bed. It was seven o'clock. Any minute now her father would be up and about and then it would be too late because he'd be bound to make her stay in and get ready for school.

She had no time to dress properly. She pulled her jeans and a thick jumper over her pyjamas, put on a thick coat and her socks and wellingtons. She slid out of the back door just as she heard her father walking across the landing to the bathroom.

Across the fields, bright and soaking with dew, by the river banks, coming out of the night into the still morning. Little birds peeped and squeaked from the rushes and willow trees; the cows stared at her across the pastures.

Amy noticed none of the stillness, her heart was in a panic. At last she came to the finger of wood where the broken oak tree lay on its side, its mountain of roots high in the air. She ran quickly round and stared up at the roots.

There in the thick clay, under the snapped and twisted tangle of roots was a long hollow. There was the print of her back, her legs, her head. At one end was a tangle of thick black hair which she had torn out in her efforts to escape. But the giant herself was gone.

Amy was filled with delight and fear. She ran around the roots but there was nothing. She should have been there to help. Had she deserted her friend? Or was the giant no friend at all . . .? Had dogs come, or people to dig her out and carry her off?

There was nothing, no sign or clue. Her fear grew. She needed to see her and touch her to know that she was truly a friend and meant no harm. She was alone with the giant but the giant wasn't there.

She climbed up the clod of roots. She could see for miles – across the long fields to where the mist gathered in a soft grey blanket, across to the young plantation of trees lying flat from the great wind. Barrow Hill floated like an island above the misty fields. She could see to the hills and to the town from up there. But there was no sign of the giant.

Now Amy began to fear that it was nothing, that it had always been nothing. Had she dreamed? Had she forgotten how to know when she was asleep and when she was awake?

At last her eye trailed down to the river bank below her. There, embedded deep in the mud by the river's edge, she saw the footprint.

There was just one, with long toes and a slender foot. Its size made it strange. It was so long, twice as long as her father's foot; it made Amy feel like a baby again, back in the days when the feet of all grown-ups were giant's feet.

Amy's head jerked round. Where was the giant?

21

'Are you there ...?' she called. Her voice rang out loudly across the quiet fields, over the water, into the mist ...

'Here ... Amy!'

For a second she clung to the roots in terror. But then she realised it was a familiar voice – her brother's. She could hear him now running along the river bank towards her. Their mother had sent him to bring her back.

As fast as she could, Amy slid down from the clod of roots. She ran round behind it out of sight and crept into one of the little pockets among the roots, where the earth had been washed away. She curled up into a ball and waited.

Peter thudded up to the fallen tree. 'Amy? Where are you? It's time for school!'

Amy curled up small like a tiny animal and held her breath.

'I know you're here, I heard you. It's stupid to hide. Mum and Dad are furious.'

Peter began to run round the roots. He stopped right by her. Amy could see his legs as he stood right next to her, turning this way and that as he peered about.

'You'll get us both into trouble!' he shouted angrily. That hurt; Amy hated to let her big brother down. She frowned furiously in her hiding place. But she wouldn't give herself up.

At last, full of threats, Peter stormed off. Amy was wise to his tricks and stayed long after he had gone ... and then come back to check up on her.

Only after he had run off a second time, and she had waited as long as she dared, did she creep out again and get on with the search.

As soon as she was out in the sunlight Amy began to panic again. Her mother and father would be out after her now. She had to find the giant and get her away and there was so little time . . . !

She ran round and round the tree, not knowing what to do. She crept down to look at the footprint again, but it was gone, raked up by Peter as he ran about looking for her. She climbed up the bank and round behind the roots to stare up at the hollow. She half believed it wouldn't be there, that she had just been dreaming awake. But there was the snapped cage of roots, broken by a terrible force. There was the torn clay and mud lying below on the grass – there was her hair torn from her when she had jerked free. Standing in the damp shadow of the earthy roots, Amy could smell the coldness of the underground. Did the giant smell like that – dead?

There was a cry from somewhere. Amy gasped, her head jerked. She'd never heard such a noise before. It wasn't speech. It sounded like a great bird calling but she had no way of knowing if it was a cry of gladness or anger or the call of a beast.

Was it calling for her?

She looked across the fields but there was nothing.

Amy began to search the ground for more footprints. She was on her own and the giant was free.

Part of her wanted to run home and escape but terrified though she was, she had come to love the silent presence waiting to be re-born from the earth.

Again the cry! Amy's head jerked, this way, that way. How that cry excited her! She searched the ground again and began to run in little circles, not sure which way to go, like a dog seeking a scent. Somewhere she could hear people calling her name. Her parents – she had to hurry. Her mind wasn't working properly. Where would the woman be? Why wasn't she here waiting? Which way would she go?

Then she realised. The giant was hiding because she must not be seen, must never be seen by anyone except Amy herself. Where could such a tall person hide? The woods; of course. She was waiting in the woods. The plantation was a little way off. Most of the trees were flat on their backs after the big wind but enough were still standing for her to hide.

Amy began to run again. She was panting, out of breath and weeping now because she was so desperate to find the giant but at the same time so frightened of finding her. She ran because she had no choice. The woman had some power over her, for good or for bad, and Amy had to go no matter what she found at the other end.

The plantation was strange. So many trees had been blown flat and they lay on the ground all pointing the same way as if a giant hand had combed or raked them flat. Some were half fallen, leaning one up against the other like wounded soldiers. The once familiar place was a battlefield.

Amy ran in between the wreckage, this way and that, panting and losing her breath. Birds jumped out from the bushes and startled her. A rabbit jumped at her feet and she thought it would burst her heart. Every tree that creaked against its neighbour, every broken twig was the giant coming upon her. Then there was a soft noise behind, like a sigh or a whisper. Amy paused. She heard the twigs bend under a great weight and turned round to see.

The giant was waiting for her among the young trees. She was as tall as they were. The sun was shining quite brightly and the leaves dappled the light on her red skin. She was maybe four metres tall – not as big as a fairy-tale giant. But it was so strange to have to look up so high to see a person that she seemed enormous. She was slim. On one side of her head her black hair was torn short and the skin was bleeding where she had ripped herself too quickly out of her clay cradle. Her face was terrible. Amy had not seen her face before. She had a snout like a dog.

She was there for Amy to see. She was so full of life she couldn't keep still but paced up and down, sniffing the air while Amy stared at her wet, twitching snout, her wide mouth, her hands lying at her sides full of strength and grace and her deep, deep eyes – huge eyes, dappled like the leaves of the wood in greens and browns. Amy could smell her. She smelt of the earth, as she had imagined, but that was just because the earth had made her so much a part of it in her long years underground. There was her real scent, too – a spicy, warm smell – like a cake baking in the oven, or a sweating horse.

Amy stared and swallowed nervously. What now? Her mind was empty with fear because although the giant was wonderful, she was frightful, too. Suddenly the face twisted. It was ghastly, it meant nothing and Amy cried out and lifted up her hand. The giant lifted her arms above her head. She opened her snout. Her teeth were like bear's teeth. And she cried out – that long, warbling note, like a bird.

Amy jumped back. The giant let her arms drop to her sides. In the distance, Amy could hear her mother and father calling her name

'What do you want?' begged Amy. 'Please ...?' She felt tears pricking her eyes.

Suddenly the giant bent forward. She took two steps. She was so fast that although Amy stumbled back she had her around her waist with her two strong hands. Amy screamed. She opened her mouth to scream again but then her breath left her as she was rushed high into the air. The giant flung her up, up like a little ball. Then she was falling and before she had a chance to yell again she was held safely, cradled in the strong arms. The long still face looked down at her. The eyes were sparkling so brightly ... and then the giant tipped back her head and again let out that high,

26

bird-like call.

The cry was still strange but now Amy knew it for what it was – a cry of pure joy at being in the sunlight, at filling her lungs with the summer air and the smell of sap and grass and growing plants. A cry of joy at being free and alive and having a friend after so long in the dead underground.

'You did it, you did it!' cried Amy. She lifted her arms and in a second the giant hugged her tightly. She didn't smile, she didn't know how, but her eyes were so bright that Amy knew she was as full of happiness at finding Amy as Amy was at finding her. Amy was like a doll in her arms. She swung her, held her, kissed her with her wet, sniffy snout, licked her ears and her face and her arms and her hands. Amy giggled and wiped the wet off her. She wrapped her arms round the giant's neck and loved her back.

They stood like that in the sunlight for a second before Amy felt a tremor go through the giant's body. Suddenly she began to run. In a second they were moving so fast they might have been in a car; but it was a silent, swift car that fled over the rough grass and hedges. Her long legs carried the giant like a deer. She could leap over the hedgerows, over the small trees or the gates and fences in a stride. They weren't going anywhere. She was running because she had to run. Her body had been so still in the cold clay for thousands of years and now she was free to move, to feel the sun on her skin, to run like the wind over the sweet grass.

27

Amy gulped at the rushing air and the world flying past. The woman threw back her head and called in her beautiful bird's voice and Amy called with her – for the sheer joy of moving, of being alive, of being together at last.

Chapter 3

Anxious not to get into trouble for not bringing his sister back, Peter made the most of his story. Anyway, Amy deserved to get into trouble for not answering him. But when he saw his parents exchange a grim look, he got scared.

'Do you think she's all right?' he asked nervously.

'You finish your breakfast and get off to school. Your father and I'll go and look for her.'

Mr Lee nodded and got up from the table, swigging back his tea. This was going to make him late for work. Peter knew it was serious then.

It was just so unlike Amy, but that wasn't the worst of it. It was that she had been calling for someone when Peter turned up – 'Are you there?' Mr and Mrs Lee had already discussed how much time their daughter was spending on her own in the meadows. Who had she gone to meet so early in the morning, when the children were all on their way to school?

Peter watched nervously from the window as his parents walked swiftly across the meadow to the river. His father in his dark business suit and glossy shoes on the green grass looked like someone from another planet. He never went on to the meadows dressed like that.

Mr and Mrs Lee walked along the river as far as

the fallen tree and beyond, calling until their voices were hoarse. But they found no trace of Amy. Now, they were really scared. Mr Lee ran back to call the police while his wife continued the search. Then he ran back out to the river to help.

Mr Lee was halfway towards the fallen oak tree when he heard a noise on the other side of the river. He turned to look ... and there was Amy. She was standing by some bushes staring sulkily at him over the water.

'Amy! Where have you been?' he demanded.

'I went for a walk,' said Amy scornfully.

Mr Lee glared at her. Had he been scared out of his wits because his daughter merely felt like a walk? Just up a few metres was a tree the storm had brought down, fallen across the river. Mr Lee got on it and gingerly balanced his way across. Amy waited crossly for him. He picked her up. She seemed all right.

'You're a bad girl,' he told her. Holding her in his arms, he carefully made his way back across the fallen tree. As soon as she got on the other side she wriggled until he put her down.

'I went for a walk,' insisted Amy in an offended voice. She turned her back on him and set off for home. Mr Lee felt his temper rise suddenly. His trouser turn-ups and his socks were soaked through with the dew. His shoes too ... he noticed for the first time they were so wet he almost had a bootful.

'You've got some questions to answer, Amy,' he told her angrily, and squelched off after her.

'I had a word with her teacher, but there doesn't seem to be any problem at school,' said Mrs Lee.

Mr Lee was sitting in the armchair watching his wife pick toys, books and other stuff off the floor. Amy was in bed. They were just waiting for Peter to finish his teeth and come for a story before he went too.

Mr Lee stretched his legs and yawned. In the morning he'd been anxious and annoyed; now he felt tired. Amy had always been an odd girl, full of strange imaginings. Over the day he'd convinced himself that it was just a game that had become too real.

'You know what she's like,' he said.

Mrs Lee pulled a face. 'She was calling to someone when Peter went for her,' she reminded him.

'She often talks out loud when she's playing,' said Mr Lee.

Mrs Lee wasn't so sure. After her husband had left for work that morning she'd done everything she could to get out of Amy what had been going on. Amy just stared at her as if she was made out of chalk, and refused even to admit she'd done anything wrong in the first place.

'I'll have a word with her tomorrow,' said Mr Lee. He got up to fetch his papers. He was tired – he was always tired after work. But he still had some paperwork to do and he'd better get it done while he still could.

'I thought you were going to read to Peter,' Mrs Lee asked him. He spread his hands helplessly. 'I've got such a lot on . . .' he begged. 'Can't you do it? I have to get this done tonight . . .'

Mrs Lee tutted.

On the other side of the door, Peter blushed angrily. They treated him like some sort of problem. Sulkily he went upstairs on his own to bed. They could come up and read to him, if they wanted. If not – see if he cared!

He often listened at the door like that to hear his parents. It was strange, listening to them on their own. Sometimes, like today, he found things out.

Like his mother, Peter wasn't so sure that everything was well with Amy. She had a secret. Maybe she had met someone in the meadows. Secrets like that were dangerous.

Peter made up his mind to find out what it was. He was interested – that was part of it. He felt left out as well. Amy always shared with him. Whatever she had, whatever she did, he was always the first one she told. Now she was on her own. And that was another thing. Peter knew his sister rather better than her parents. His guess was that Amy was frightened.

As he lay in bed, feet sounded on the stairs. His mother. Peter waited. She went to the toilet, then walked down the corridor. She paused outside his door, listening.

Peter opened his mouth to call her, but he closed it before he said anything. He wanted her to come in on her own. For half a minute, mother and son listened to one another being quiet on the other side of the door. Then Mary Lee told herself he didn't care and walked on. Peter almost called her as she walked past, but he was too proud.

He glared at the ceiling and beat his bedclothes. He wanted his story and a hug but it was too late now.

Later on, when he could hear the telly on downstairs, Peter slid out of bed and crept across the landing and into Amy's room.

It was dark in there. At first he thought she was still asleep but as he walked towards her she sat up suddenly. 'Is it you?' she begged.

She sounded as if she was expecting someone. In the darkness Peter waited until Amy fumbled with the light switch. Her eyes stared brightly at him.

'It's you,' she said. She lay back down.

'What's wrong, Amy?' begged Peter.

Amy said nothing but lay on the bed staring at the wall, waiting for him to go away. Peter came and sat on the bed, inflamed with curiosity.

'Tell me,' he whispered. Amy didn't move. 'Did you really pretend to be sick to get off school?' he asked in admiration. Amy looked at him and began to smile, but then looked away.

'Go away,' she told him.

Peter was hurt. 'I won't be your friend,' he threatened. Normally that was enough to make Amy do anything at all. But now she didn't care. Peter bent closer.

'I always keep secrets, don't I?' he begged. Amy

33

didn't respond. He tried a different way. 'You know you shouldn't play with strangers, don't you, Amy?' he said cunningly.

Amy looked at him in alarm. 'I don't know any strangers,' she said, and Peter felt a little thrill of fear go through him. He'd got it right – there was a stranger! She had met someone down by the meadows after all. But why should it be a secret? What had this person got to hide?

'You know you shouldn't, Amy,' he told her. 'It's dangerous to talk with strangers. You have to tell Mum and Dad.'

Amy hunched her shoulders. She wanted to tell so much. She would have loved to tell Peter so that he would admire her for the wonderful things she had known and understood, for the way she had helped the giant out of the earth and made friends with her. But her new friend had won over her soul and mind and she knew she could never do anything the giant didn't want.

'I can't tell . . . anyone . . .' she began.

'You have to tell!' exclaimed Peter greedily. 'Secrets can be dangerous, you know,' he added quickly, seeing that he'd shut her up. Amy turned to look at him, her face bright with anger that he was making her talk about it.

'It's not for you,' she told him. She laid her head down on the pillow. 'Go to bed,' she said. She snuggled down under the blankets and wished him away.

Peter paused. 'Good night,' he said at last, and bent down to kiss her. She glanced at him in surprise because he never did that. Peter left the room. He had surprised himself. He had been greedy for the secret but the way Amy spoke frightened him. She seemed like another person altogether.

When Peter shut the door and left her on her own, Amy closed her eyes and willed herself to sleep. It was no use of course; she was far too excited.

Amy had no idea how she understood her new friend, who never spoke. But she did understand everything. Not in words, but how she felt, what she needed. Now she understood that the giant woman had to hide. The wild run across the fields earlier had ended suddenly when they came across a tractor chugging across the meadows. Amy felt the surge of fear under her ribs and knew that was how the giant felt. To be caught . . . That would be the most dreadful thing of all.

The giant had dived quickly down under a hedge and lay close to the ground trembling, until the sound of the engine faded. Then she picked herself up and made her way back to the river, bowed low, sometimes on her hands and knees to be sure she was out of sight. For all her size she was trembling like a scared mouse.

'That was silly!' scolded Amy, realising how dreadfully stupid the run had been. The urge to move had been too much after being still so long.

To be seen would be the end, the very end. A long time ago the giant had been seen. Then she had been hunted and injured and had had to return to the earth to sleep and to heal and wait all over again. She could not bear the thought of such a thing happening again. She was sure she would die if it happened again.

Amy did not understand any details but she understood very well that something the giant had waited for for a very long time was soon to happen. It was terribly important that she did not miss it again. Meanwhile, she had to be safely hidden away before any harm came to her.

Amy knew just the place.

Much later, Amy awoke. She knew that the giant had left her hiding place in the woods beyond the pasture and had begun to move across the fields towards the river. Amy knew, not with her mind but with her heart, her bones, her blood. She knew when the giant began to follow the river's silver and dark trail under the moon. She could feel the black fields, see the row of lights from the houses of Amy's road. Amy sensed the call of a fox in the darkness, felt the recognition – this was something the giant had known before. A light appeared in the meadow. The giant crouched down low amongst the trees while a man passed, an angler out for some night-time fishing. Amy felt her confusion and fear at the light, at the man behind it, at the sound of cars on the distant main road – all unknown things.

And now the woman was walking across the grass towards Amy's house. How quickly she crossed the still pasture! Now she was stepping over the stile and standing, marked with moonlight, in the garden. Amy felt a bolt of fear that her parents might open the curtains and peer out and see what they never should see. Her parents were long in bed but the giant felt her fear and hurriedly crossed the lawn to hide in the deep shadows close to the side of the house. Then she came round to the back. Now, at this very moment, she was watching Amy's window.

With a squeal of pleasure Amy got out of bed and ran to open the window. From the shadows, her long face expressionless, her anxiety beating in Amy's own chest, the tall figure like a dream moved across the drive. She came to stand under Amy's window and held up her arms, inviting her to jump. Amy climbed up onto the sill, her legs dangling down, and let herself drop safely into the waiting arms.

'You're frozen!' she exclaimed crossly as the giant held her close. The giant held her and nuzzled her against her cold cheek. Her friend was naked, she realised for the first time. She thought of the covers on her bed. But the woman made a curious movement with her head. It meant, 'No.' Amy watched, entranced by the long face, the deep eyes. That snout! It was wet, and twitchy, always sniffing and moving as she tasted the air with it. But Amy was getting used to it. It was part of her face. She was beautiful.

The giant turned and took long steps onto the road.

37

They had gone no more than a few steps when a car turned into their road. With a gasp the giant slid quickly away to the side of the house and pressed herself against the wall while the bright lights drove past. Her nose sniffed at the acrid fumes and she made a little snort of disgust. The deep of the late night fell again. The giant sighed and shuddered. Now the danger was greatest. She had left the safety of the earth and was not yet hidden in her waiting place – like a crab that had shed its shell and had to wait soft and helpless until the new one grew.

Anxiously, the giant peered around the wall and glanced this way, that way, to see if the road was clear. Then she stepped back into the shadows behind the house and headed back to the fields.

They would take the long way, the still way, into town.

The dark shapes of the trees and the moonlight-dappled river flashed past. Further out, beyond the hedgerows, the lights of the town slowly advanced. Amy clung to the giant's neck like a monkey. She could see nothing in the darkness but the giant seemed to know where everything was. Amy gulped the cold air. She could feel the giant's heart beating, her skin grow hot as she ran. She ran like the wind, full of joy. Once she leapt over the wide river in a single bound. But despite her terrific speed, she never even stumbled.

When they got to town, everything slowed down.

They stepped over a tall fence onto a tree-dotted road with rows of terraced houses on either side. Further down the street were a couple of lights on in the upstairs windows, even at this late hour. Still cars lined the road, looking muddy orange in the street lamps. The giant hunched her shoulders and began to creep swiftly down the street. Amy remembered the factory yard a hundred metres further on. The giant was reading Amy's mind. She did not know what she was looking for, but the feeling – a safe place where she could pause and hide – came over loud and clear.

They made the factory safely and the giant gratefully slid in between the dark buildings. Then a dog barked. Her heart jumped in terror. How could she forget that terrible noise, those terrible creatures with their claws and teeth? Without thinking she started out and began to run down the road full tilt.

Amy cried out. This was terrible! The giant was in a mad panic. She had no idea that the dogs were safely locked up. Now she would certainly be seen. But after a swift dash the giant understood. She froze, suddenly aware of the danger she had put herself in.

For a second she stood recovering in the road. In this world there was danger everywhere for her. Now the noise of a car; and the street was flooded with light as the machine came towards them. There seemed nowhere to hide and Amy was certain they'd be caught but the giant stepped in one long stride over the pavement, over a low wall at the edge of someone's garden – quick as a tiger. Already they were down flat on the ground. The giant curled up in a ball on her side among the thorny rose bushes that grew there. There was a terrible moment when it seemed that the car was pausing . . . but then the engine revved and it sped away.

'It's all right . . . really, it's all right. We're nearly there,' encouraged Amy. But the giant lay shivering. She was gasping. She hid her face in her hands and began to moan with fear. She was so helpless here. She was terrified.

Amy felt her fear, shared it and suddenly began to cry. She would have done anything for her friend, but she couldn't bear feeling so much fear.

For a moment the giant looked curiously at her, then she touched her eyes gently with a finger and licked her tears. She seemed to pull herself together. She cradled Amy and tried to make her face into the expression of pleasure for these people – a smile. Her face wasn't used to it of course; it looked like a sneer. But she wanted to comfort her and sensing that, Amy was comforted. They cuddled and stroked each other. Then the giant stood up and made her way up the road.

At last the dark shape of the big building Amy was looking for loomed up before them. The Roxy – the old cinema. Last year it had closed down. One day they would knock it down, probably. Now, boarded-up and still, it stood empty, dark, silent, huge – the very place to hide a giant.

They prowled like mice about the ground around the building. Every door, every window was boarded up with thick plyboard. They went round once, twice. There was no way in.

In front of the entrance, the steps were covered overhead so that people could shelter before the doors opened. Above was the space used to advertise the films in tall black letters. Above that, far above, was a long row of tall windows. When she had been inside to see a film Amy used to look out of them from the inside and see far across the town. Now, below on the ground, Amy remembered how different the town looked from up there. She saw the giant's head turn up.

'You can't get up there . . .' she began. But her words were cut short as the giant took her by the waist and the air vanished from her mouth as she swooped up high once more. The giant reached leisurely up with her impossibly long arm until her hand was resting on the long ledge above the steps, and she bounded up. Suddenly they were high above the ground. Next to them were the giant letters of the last film the cinema had shown – 'Jurassic Park'. Up here, close to them, the letters were as big as dinosaurs themselves.

The giant could climb like an ape. A couple of leaps and swoops from ledge to ledge, from window to window, and they already stood on a narrow ledge right under the rows of windows high in the building. The windows always used to remind Amy

41

of eyes when she saw them from the ground but now they, too, were boarded up. Amy groaned with disappointment.

The giant placed Amy at her feet. Amy looked down. In the dark the distance was hidden. Above her, the giant had taken hold of one of the big pieces of plyboard that covered the row of windows. She pulled. There was a long, groaning squeak as the nails moved out of the wood. She removed the boarding and put it carefully to one side. She covered her face with her arm, held the other long hand like an umbrella over Amy and with a sudden movement of her elbow smashed the small pane of glass at the top. Now she could put her arm in to open the window.

The part of the window that opened was small; Amy was certain it was too small for any giant – even a fairly small one like her friend. But the giant seemed to be double jointed on top of everything else. She folded herself in two and stepped neatly through the little space. Then she reached over and lifted Amy in after her. Finally she reached out, took the board lying on the ledge outside, and pulled it back firmly into place.

Inside it was dark, darker than anywhere Amy had ever been before. At first there were thin streaks of dull lamplight from the street below coming in past the plyboard nailed tightly to the windows. But when they went down the stairs into the auditorium, there were no windows at all. The darkness was almost solid. It was like being draped in something thick and black. Amy kept putting her hand out, as if she could actually bump into the darkness and hurt her nose.

It smelt bad, not like Amy remembered it – of damp creeping into the cushions, of air trapped in the building where the doors were never opened – as if the air itself had begun to rot. The giant held Amy close in her arms as she explored. Despite her good night-eyes, she too was blind in the total darkness and had to feel her way forward . . . round the seats, down the corridors.

No one ever came into the deserted cinema. Amy had chosen well for her friend, but it was a heavy price for the giant to pay. She had been so long underground; she had so much loved the outside. Now she was to be buried again in the dark.

The giant sat on the carpet, her back against the wall, and bowed her head. Amy cradled her and kissed her.

She felt the great eyes grow wet.

'You can cry . . .' she murmured, almost in delight, because the giant was not human. The way her face worked, the way her feelings moved inside Amy as well as herself, these things made her so different. But she had tears for sadness just like we do, and Amy loved her for it.

The two, the giant and the little girl, curled up together on the carpet in the foyer of the cinema. They leaned against the wall and waited a while in the darkness, to be together. In such darkness, with the warmth of the giant creeping into her, Amy felt so peaceful. She could almost be at home in her mother's bed. She began to doze. Her head was resting on the giant's stomach with the slow, steady beat of her heart softly counting time. Sleepily she listened. It was not the double beat . . . ba-boom, ba-boom, of a human heart. Ba-ba-ba-boom, ba-ba-ba-boom it went.

Whatever else the giant was, she was not merely a big person.

Amy sat up. 'I have to go now,' she said awkwardly. The giant sighed; she was scared of being on her own. But she picked Amy up like a doll and began carefully stepping through the seats. They left the auditorium and walked along a corridor until they came to a place where the windows showed thin lines of lamplight from outside. The giant paused and listened intently, before breaking the glass in one of the windows. The brittle crash and shattering seemed to fill the whole night and they waited quietly again afterwards, but no one came. Then, the giant placed one of her long, beautiful hands on the plyboard and pushed it away from the window, so there was enough space for Amy to creep through.

Amy squeezed half out. She was coming out into the alleyway by the side of the cinema. She glanced back. The long red face looked back at her.

'I'll try and come back,' said Amy awkwardly, not knowing if she had done everything she should have. 'Maybe I can get a light . . . a torch or something. Candles? Do you know fire?' she added, because the giant from the earth seemed to know so little. 'And some food,' she added. 'You'll have to have some food, won't you?'

The giant moved her mouth. It looked awful when that ferocious snout twisted like that and despite herself Amy gasped and took a step back. The big face swooped towards her. She kissed Amy quickly on the cheek. Then she stepped quickly back into the building.

'Goodbye,' Amy said. The giant pulled the plywood closed. The nails groaned back into place. Amy heard her move away up the corridor. She was alone. She turned to peer out onto the road.

Amy stood still a while as it sank in. She knew well enough how dangerous it was for the giant to come into the open. Amy had to find her own way back. She was not so very far away from home, she knew her way.

But it was so dark . . .

Then Amy realised that actually she was not alone at all. Inside her, sharing her fears, thoughts, her every step, was her friend the giant. She shared in Amy's mind, just as Amy shared hers. In the dark, on her own, it made no difference. Amy would never be alone again until the giant left her alone.

Cautiously, Amy began to move out of the alleyway. On the road there were streetlamps, but that just meant she could be seen. It would be better to go round, to get off the road and go by the fields as the giant had done. But Amy was frightened of the dark. For a moment she stood undecided. She thought she was going to cry. But that would never do because then her friend would know and might come to help her and that was dangerous. Bunching her courage up, she made a dash for the road.

Despite the reassuring presence inside, it was a dreadful journey. Once she saw a man, swaying along the road. He looked terrible and huge in the dark. She hid behind a car until he was past and then continued on her way.

The little girl ran alone up the deserted streets, past the still cars and the sleeping houses. Gradually the fear of it wore off and she was filled with a fierce excitement . . . because she was so brave to be out alone, because she had a secret no one in the world knew, because there were difficult things she'd had to do for her friend and she'd done them. Her house came into sight. Amy stopped running and began to walk, she was so sure of herself. She would come again she promised herself. As often as she could, she would walk alone in the dark streets to visit her new friend.

Chapter 4

In the couple of weeks that followed, all the excitement caused by Amy's skipping off school died down. She stopped hanging about by the river meadows altogether. It was as if her secret, whatever it was, had scared her as much as it had scared the rest of the family, and she had just dropped it. She played all day with Peter, following him about until she drove him mad. She seemed often tired, despite early nights, that was the only odd thing. Mrs Lee gave her vitamins every morning, kept her eye on her, and took her husband's advice to stop worrying.

Peter was still curious. He questioned her from time to time, but Amy just wandered off and got cross if he went on about it. He noticed often a strange, anxious look on her face. But it very quickly became just another part of his little sister's dreamy ways. He didn't worry about it until one night when he discovered that her secret was leading her to do things he would never have dared himself.

He was awake suddenly. It was very dark and still. He had no idea what woke him up. All he knew was that he was suddenly open eyed and wide awake in his bed.

Something had happened – something unex-

47

pected and out of place. He lay very still but he heard nothing. He glanced at the clock on the wall but it was too dark to see anything. That meant it was horribly early. He turned over and pulled the covers up to his neck.

Then he heard someone cross the carpet on the landing outside his door.

Whoever it was, they were being quiet. They began to creep downstairs; Peter knew the third stair from the creak it always made. The person paused, listened in case someone had heard. He knew at once it was Amy.

Sometimes Amy walked in her sleep. There was the time they found her making sandwiches out of slices of cake and piccalilli at three o'clock in the morning. She'd woken up when they came down and claimed she was doing it on purpose. She tried to eat the sandwiches for breakfast but they tasted so disgusting she had to give up.

That had been funny. Other times had been different, like the time Peter woke up and looked out of his window at two in the morning to see his sister standing in her pyjamas and bare feet on the concrete drive with the frost in her hair. Her toes were blue, she had frost on the nails but she hadn't cared at the time. Only later when she woke up she cried, her feet hurt so much.

Peter was scared but excited when he heard her pause on the third stair to listen and see if anyone had heard her. That meant she wasn't asleep. Peter knew at once – this was her secret.

48

He waited until he was sure she was downstairs before he crept out of bed and opened his door.

The hall lights were off but he could see the lights from the kitchen shining under the door. Perhaps it was nothing. She might be getting a drink of juice or something. But then he heard the back door go.

'She's gone out,' he thought. Although he'd been expecting something he was so surprised he just stood there dumbly for a second. His timid sister going out alone in the deep dead of night? As he stood, he felt his heart speed up. He ought to go to his parents . . . after that time in the frost they'd made him swear he'd fetch them if he saw anything like it again.

Peter wasn't all that used to doing as he was told. 'You're too wild!' they all said to him. He was proud of that but a bit ashamed too. He knew it was dangerous for his sister to go out alone . . . come to that it was dangerous for him at this time of night.

But this was an adventure.

Peter was sure of one thing. If she was brave enough to go out on her own, so was he. Besides . . . he wanted that secret.

He ran quietly to his window at the front just in time to see Amy walk round the side of the house. She was wrapped up with a coat and woolly hat on as if it was the middle of winter, although it was July. She carried a bag in her hand. Just before she began up the drive she turned and cast an anxious look back over her shoulder up at the house. Peter darted back into the shadows. He was certain she wasn't sleepwalking now. That alert, quick look had nothing of sleep about it. As fast as he could he pulled on his jeans and a thick sweater over his pyjamas, and ran downstairs.

On the road he hid behind the privet hedge and glanced up and down but he couldn't see her. Hurriedly he ran as quickly and as quietly as he could after her, pausing every now and then to peer ahead. At first he thought he'd missed her. But he saw a small figure up the road, crouching low by the side of a still car. She was peering behind her. Her face was white. Peter darted behind a car himself.

In a second Amy hurried on her way. Peter waited, and then followed on up the deserted street.

This was terrifying. The houses and trees, the familiar turns in the road all looked like ghosts, lifelessly waiting for something to happen. The street lights shone for no one. Peter was scared of his sister, as if she, too, were a ghost. But he was on his way now. He stayed behind, out of sight, and followed Amy into town.

They came to the local shops. Here there were one or two people still about on the street. A couple walked rapidly past.

Amy saw them first, and dived behind a low wall. Peter got behind a hedge. Standing still, he shivered. He'd thought it would be warm, being summer, but at this hour of night it was cold. The couple walked past but before he could get out a man came up from behind and he had to wait in his hiding place while he passed. The man crossed the road and disappeared down a side alley. When Peter looked out again, Amy had disappeared.

He ran quietly forward. He had to hide again when a police car appeared, cruising slowly through the streets. When it went he ran on again, fearing to go too fast or make too much noise in case she was still in hiding nearby. But this time there was no little figure hurrying through the streets, no quick patter of footsteps on the pavement.

Amy had disappeared.

Peter stared desperately round him – he couldn't lose her! He would be to blame if anything happened to her, he should have stopped her or fetched his parents. He ran desperately up and down and looked at the side roads but he could see nothing.

Peter was standing by the side of an old building – the old Roxy cinema. A couple of years ago his parents used to take him and Amy. Now it was still and dark. It looked as if it had been blinded with those boards over its windows and doors. It was getting shabby and old. Rubbish drifted around its tall walls.

A dark, dirty alley ran up one side. It never occurred to Peter that she might have hidden in there; it was just too frightening. It was so dark. No street lights shone down the narrow line of old boxes, rubbish and dustbins.

But he heard a noise. Peter slid out of his hiding place behind a telephone box and peered round the corner into the dark alley just in time to see the little

51

form of his sister, fat in her coat and scarf, crouching halfway down. She paused, looked quickly up and down . . . and then to his horror disappeared into the side of the building.

Peter couldn't believe what she was doing. Every moment, it got worse. He waited a second and then tiptoed down the alley after her.

The alley was horrible, it was all darkness. There were so many dirty places where ghosts and men might hide. He squeezed past the dustbins, squeezed around a pile of rubbish tumbling out of cardboard boxes. To one side was a slight noise. Peter hid behind a box and peeped out. There was a tall board nailed to a side door. But one side of the board had been pulled away. He could see the long nails shining dully. Behind the gap was a deep, thick blackness, empty of any light or shape.

He thought . . . she can't have gone down there?

But she had. She had walked into that throat of darkness. Now he heard noises. Peter got closer. He listened hard.

He could hear long steps. The floor creaked slowly under some great weight. Something was in there with her.

Peter wanted to call her . . . 'Amy!' . . . but that could be dangerous, for the – whatever it was – would hear him. He should go and get help, of course. But . . .

Amy had gone in. It was like a dare. It was simply not possible for his little sister to be braver than him. He didn't have to go right in but . . . just a few steps. Just enough to taste the darkness and show her ...

Peter bit his lip, held his breath, and squeezed in the gap after her.

The first thing was the smell. There was the smell of the cinema of course – the smell of dampness and trapped air. But there was something else – a rich, animal smell, like the smell of the big animals in the circus, when he'd been to see them in their pens before the show. But it was spicy, as if someone had sprinkled cinnamon amongst the straw.

Ahead of him were noises – soft noises. There were Amy's feet. Her voice, whispering ...

'I know I shouldn't come, but I have to, don't I?' she was whispering.

There was no reply but Peter was certain he heard a long slow breath, like a sigh. Too long. It might have been a horse sighing. Or a lion. The floor creaked again under that weight, and the great crea-ture – he felt certain it was no person – moved away into the building.

Peter held tightly to the wooden frame of the door. He felt dizzy. He was freezing cold and scared out of his wits.

Amy was with a monster.

And yet ... although his senses told him that there was some great creature in there ... he didn't believe it. The darkness plays tricks. What you can't see, you imagine. Besides, Peter didn't believe in monsters. So what could it be? A horse, for heaven's sake? In a cinema? A lion? It was such nonsense! It was the stuff of fairy tales, and Peter was too old for fairy tales.

It must be a person. More dangerous than any lion.

Peter began to see that the darkness wasn't complete. Light was finding its way in through the cracks between the hoardings, just narrow slits of dullness against the black. They were in a corridor. Peter thought he'd go just to the end of it, far enough to peep through the door and see if there was any light beyond. Just enough to glimpse what was really there.

He inched forward. He was terrified he'd make a noise and give himself away. He kept peering back over his shoulder so as not to lose sight of that precious pale gap to the outside world behind him. So long as he kept the way out in sight he could make a run for it.

He had to feel his way along the walls. At last he got to the door. He held tightly onto the frame and poked his head through.

The darkness was so thick he felt it would get up his nose and in his mouth. It was like dipping his head into some liquid. He pulled it out again at once. He peered this way and that before he plunged his head back in. He blinked his eyes. He could see nothing, not the frame of the door he was holding onto, not his hands, not the nose on his face. He blinked again, waiting for his eyes to get used to it and show him something. But there was nothing. That lightless space might have been as small as a cupboard or as vast as a cathedral; there were no clues.

He heard Amy somewhere in the endless darkness chattering away in a half whisper. 'Do you like apples?' she said. 'You should use the torch,' she added. 'No one will see at this time of night.' Whoever it was did not reply but Peter could hear the soft footsteps, long and heavy. There was a brushing, sliding sound, as if the thing was holding its hand against the wall as it walked down the cinema.

Peter thought of monsters in the dark – of minotaurs and gorgons, of trolls and giants and ogres. Maybe Amy had never seen the thing she had made friends with. Maybe it only met her in the darkness. It had told her it was beautiful and she didn't realise what a monster she was with. Or had Amy made friends with something that had escaped from one of the films they used to show?

Peter peered over his shoulder. Behind him, like a pale beacon, was a dull strip of light, the way out to the world of school and grown-ups and sense, some way off now.

So long as he could see that, he was safe.

Peter walked inside. He kept hold of the door frame. He could still see the way out. Then, just to prove to himself that he could do it ... that he would still be there when the darkness was total, Peter crept round the corner until the way out was hidden. Now he was truly floating in blackness. He let go of the wall. He was relieved to find he was still himself.

'I tried to get some bread but it was all frozen,' explained Amy matter-of-factly, further down the cinema. Was it a dream? Peter moved up a few feet and then, for his final dare – it really was his final dare this time – he took four steps out from the wall into the darkness, into the emptiness where there might have been a sheer drop of a thousand feet right there at his toes, for all he knew.

Something struck his shins. Peter gasped and snatched in fear of falling. He lost his balance and fell. He cried out and fell heavily onto velvet seats.

The darkness throbbed with shock. A giant throat cried out – a strange, empty call like a wounded bird; a giant bird; a monster.

Peter jumped to his feet, he made a dash for the door. He fell again. It was the cinema seats; he seemed to have fallen right among them, they were all around him. He fought his way over them, through them, fought his way to the narrow aisle. He was crashing, banging. He had to get out now – quick. But the seats were going on forever, they were on all sides.

He had lost himself. The darkness seized him – seamless, endless, without shape or colour or line. He had no idea which way to go.

Suddenly he stepped backwards into the aisle. He was confused – it seemed to have moved. Was it the same aisle?

Something big was moving fast towards him in

the darkness. He could hear the long feet beating on the carpet, the breath of it. It would be here in seconds. His nostrils were filled with the spicy, sweaty scent. Everything was so vast in the darkness and there was still no sight of the chink of light that led back to the world where everything was safe and real.

Peter found the wall. He fumbled along it looking for the door. It should have been here but it wasn't; it should be over there but it wasn't. His hand banged something down – a picture? No, it was the door frame . . . and there at the end of the corridor was the seam of light that led to safety.

But it was too late. The ground shook under him. The scent of straw and animal and spice filled his nostrils. Peter screamed once and fled – away from the beast, away from the light, into the terror of the darkness, where he might hide. Behind him, the beast paused at the doorway to listen, and then gave chase.

Peter was certain it would catch him, but he had a strange kind of luck. He wasn't running straight up the aisle. He fell over into the seats and then he was crawling, climbing, swimming over them. He fell to the floor and an instinct made him lie perfectly still. His heart was climbing up his throat, his breath was hoarse and loud. He held his breath. He could hear the monster standing nearby, listening.

He waited, tried not to cry and yell. The monster began to pace to and fro, up and down. It began to climb over the seats towards him. He had to stay still!

The smell was overpowering. It was standing right by him. He could hear sniffing. It was tasting and testing the air. It could smell him! The old rhyme ran through his mind: 'I smell the blood of an Englishman ... I'll grind his bones to make my bread.' His muscles tried to jerk and run but he forced himself to stay still. At last, the huge presence withdrew. Peter heard it step over the seats to the aisle. He was certain it had two legs.

He had no idea what to do ... what could he do, but keep still? From out of the darkness to the right he heard a strange noise – a wrenching, squeaking noise. Peter guessed what it was at once. The monster was closing the gap to the outside. That sound was the nails going home into the wood, the thick plyboard pushing back onto the frame. Peter was trapped.

He lay face down on the floor for what seemed like hours until the beast came back. This time it had light.

Peter saw the beam of the torch flying across the walls. It was still some way from him. Peeping sideways he could see where he was at last – the high ceiling and walls, the rows and rows of seating, the blank screen. There were a number of doors around the big hall. Which of them, if any, led to escape?

Silently he got to his hands and knees and peeped over the top of the seats to see what was happening.

At first he thought it was some mad woman. She was dressed in some strange cloth, draped over her and around her. Her hair was tatty. She was a funny colour. She was bending down low – too low, he thought vaguely – and shining the beam of her torch in her hand up the aisles one at a time. She was working her way towards him.

Peter was so relieved to see it was just a person. People were dangerous sometimes, he knew that, but at least it wasn't a nightmare come true. Then he saw his sister run up to the woman.

The woman peered at her as she came. Amy was crying and pulling at the cloth, but the woman brushed her lightly away with her hand.

Peter's face fell. Amy came to just above her knee. It was a giant. The woman was a giant. She was huge. She was a giant.

He must have made some noise because she looked straight at him. Peter saw her face.

He screamed. It was all up now. It was true, it was a monster; he'd stopped believing in them but here it was and it was after him – really, truly after his blood. He couldn't run, he was falling over the seats. The beam of light swung at him, trapped him like an insect. He was falling, screaming, yelling. He clutched his head and howled. Now he was out of the seats, crawling up the aisle. He got up and ran into a wall and bloodied his nose. By the light shining on his back he could see a door in front of him; he went for it.

Through the door. The darkness again. It was going to catch him in the dark. It was getting close. He heard Amy yell and he screamed back at her to help him but he didn't stop running. He fell. Behind him the door opened but there was no light. He groped with his hands. He was half lying on stairs. He was flying up the stairs. He was screaming Amy's name. It was dark again. He was banging into walls. He thought of a mouse he had cornered at home once; he was like that. Suddenly he was in a big open space again and his senses returned, enough for him to keep his mouth shut again. But he didn't stop running. Nothing now could ever stop him running.

As soon as Giant heard the noise and cried out, Amy felt a pulse of terrible fear. Then, rage. This came from Giant. Amy understood at once that her friend would do anything to anyone rather than get caught.

Amy ran to hide under a seat by the screen. She was appalled. Before there had been fear, but always tenderness with it. Now all this was blazed away in a blast of hatred. Giant was turning into a monster before her eyes. Only when the boy cried out and Amy realised that it was her brother who was being hunted, did she run out from her hiding-place and try to stop Giant.

She came full pelt up the carpeted aisle towards the beam of light that trapped her brother like a moth. Giant turned as she caught up with her and

Amy seized her cloak and began screaming: 'Run Peter, run, run!' She climbed up Giant like a fierce, small animal. The tall woman stood and watched in amazement as Amy clawed her way up to her waist and seized the torch. She dangled for a moment by both hands. Then Giant let go and Amy crashed down to the floor with the torch triumphantly in her hands.

'Run Peter, run!' she screamed again, making off back down the aisle before Giant could get her. She heard Peter screaming her name in a voice she had never heard from him before. He was in total panic. She turned but Giant had already made off after him in the dark. Amy turned off the light. She held her breath and listened to the unequal hunt in the cinema dark . . . the terrified boy and the desperate giant, both blind with darkness. Peter was screaming and screaming. There was a thud as he hit a wall. In the moment of silence that followed, she could clearly hear Giant sniffing the air.

Peter crashed violently out of the doors at the back of the cinema. She could hear his screams muffled on the stairs. A moment later, still screaming hoarsely, he emerged through the balcony doors above. Amy called his name once more and he stopped screaming, but he still charged blindly forward, crashing over the seats, falling, gasping. Giant on the other hand was keeping a deadly silence. Amy had no idea where she was.

The noises stopped above her. Amy held her breath and stared up. She could hear little noises and his ragged breath.

'Peter . . .' she said softly. He answered with a sobbing wail.

What was happening? Amy wrapped her fingers round the torch, looking for the switch. She turned it on and shone the beam up.

There was the ceiling with its ornate golden carvings. There was the lip of the balcony. And there, right on the edge, on his knees, inches from the deadly fall, his hands reaching in front of him like a blind beetle feeling in space, was her brother.

She screamed . . . 'Peter . . .!' He jerked as her voice split the darkness. His hands clawed the air. He tottered over the emptiness, lashed the air with his arms, screamed, and fell like a stone.

Chapter 5

There were flickering candles. It was warm. There was Amy's face bent carefully over him, tear-stained. A dream? It had to have been a dream, because it had been a fairy tale but real.

Then he saw it. It was sitting behind Amy not looking at him but examining its arms. It was dressed in the strange blue garment he'd seen it in before. Now he recognised what it was. The monster had dressed itself in the curtain that used to hang across the big screen.

It could almost have been a woman but it was so big and its face was so still and deformed, it was more than half an animal.

Peter began to whimper and cringe away but the pain in his back and legs made him cry out.

The giant looked his way. Its face, its deep eyes that were so big even for her, seemed to soak him up. Then the lips twisted. It was a snarl.

'You shouldn't have come,' Amy scolded. 'You nearly ruined everything. I told you no one was to know.' But she was smiling. Amy was glad she had someone to share her secret with. It had been too much for her, all on her own.

She saw him looking anxiously at Giant. 'Giant's my friend. She saved you,' she said. 'She caught you. I thought she was going to get you but she saved you instead!' Her face beamed with pleasure and pride. 'Look . . .' She stepped back and held Giant's hand to show Peter her arms. They were bright red and already turning black with bruises. She was strong, but not superhuman. An ordinary person would have been flattened by the weight of the boy falling so far. The giant had broken his fall, but she was lucky not to have broken her bones at the same time.

Peter barely took any of this in. As he came out of his faint the shock returned. His teeth began to chatter, he began to sweat, he tried to edge further away.

'Don't be scared,' scolded Amy. She grinned. She was so pleased that she wasn't afraid and Peter was! 'She's my friend . . . our friend,' she offered.

The giant came over. She sat on the floor by Peter's side, nursing her bruised arms. Peter began to pant with fear. By the light of the candle he watched her face. That snout, those huge jaws – an animal's jaws. Her lips twisted again into that ferocious expression. He cried out.

'She's smiling,' said Amy crossly. 'Don't you know a smile? But she's not very good at it,' she added. 'She doesn't use her face like we do. She's only doing it for you . . . to show you she's friendly, aren't you, Giant?'

The giant nodded her head. Peter looked closely. Yes, it might be a smile. But it could as easily be a snarl.

'Giant – is that her name?' he asked.

'That's what I call her.'

'Why doesn't she talk?' he wanted to know.

'She can't talk. I don't think she knows English.'

Peter swallowed. Amy was so easy with the monster! The monster had fooled Amy. It would be better for him if he pretended to be fooled too.

He wondered if she was a French giant.

'*Parlez-vous français*?' he asked her, nodding brightly.

The giant looked steadily at him, and then at Amy.

'She hardly ever says anything,' said Amy. 'She was buried in the ground for thousands of years so I don't suppose they used to talk like we do, then. She was under that tree – the old tree by the river. I knew, you see. It's my secret!' She suddenly clutched Peter's arm and smiled wickedly. Yes, she had known. It was magic. Peter looked curiously at her, and then at the giant. What did this creature want with his sister?

'Isn't she beautiful?' said Amy proudly.

Yes, she was beautiful. Her still face was like the face of a statue. When you looked closely that alarming snout and those great yellow teeth were part of her beauty. Her skin shone in the candle-light. Her wide mouth was still, her lips only opened when she sighed. Her deep, deep eyes were full of colours and life. They were quick, like water.

Peter stared. It was impossible but there she was. Not a person – you could tell that easily enough. Something else altogether.

He leaned across to Amy and whispered, as if the woman could understand. 'What's she doing here?'

'She's waiting,' said Amy. 'Only, I don't know what for.'

Peter stared at the giant, unable to understand her. She stared back, unable to understand him.

Maybe she was a German giant. He didn't know German except for the one phrase . . . '*Sprechen Sie Deutsch*?' he asked.

The giant only stared. Then he gasped in fright – but she was only lifting her arms. She placed her crossed hands on her heart and then reached her hands towards him as if she was handing him her heart – as if by this gesture she could cross the huge gulf of thousands of years and more between them. Then she settled herself down on her haunches, still watching him.

She opened her mouth and began to sing.

It was no song heard on earth before. The tune was no tune, the words no language. Her voice was like the voice of a bird and of a girl and of an instrument. Parts of it were not beautiful. It was surprising. Sometimes she clapped her hands. Sometimes she shook her head to fling her voice around or rattled her fingers together. Her voice was a kind of chorus.

There was a long pause when it was over.

'She never did that before,' said Amy in an awed voice.

The giant looked at them . . . anxiously? Friendlily? Greedily? There was no way of knowing. Her lips began to twist again. She was so clumsy. Suddenly in a little gesture of impatience she grabbed hold of her mouth in her fingers and twisted the edges upwards in a smile, nodding at the two children eagerly.

'She's found a way of smiling!' exclaimed Peter, and he laughed.

'That's the best way for you to smile,' giggled Amy. It was funny – holding her mouth because she didn't know how to smile. Giant's shoulders began to go up and down and she made a funny huffing noise, almost silent.

'Look, that's her laugh,' explained Amy. But Peter was shocked – it looked too much like something dangerous. So Giant grabbed her lips and made an unhappy face, and he burst out laughing again.

Amy said, 'She wants you to help her.'

Peter stopped laughing and stared. Giant had made him laugh and she had made that strange and wonderful music. But she was so big – so different. He could understand nothing – not what she thought, or felt, or wanted.

The giant was dangerous.

'We'd better get home now,' he told Amy. He tried to get up and winced.

Amy jumped up. 'But what are we going to tell Mum and Dad?' she begged. 'About you being hurt? You'll have to think of a story – think of a story, Peter.'

Peter nodded his head. 'On the way home,' he said. He would have said anything he had to.

Peter had to clutch at the walls and hobble as he walked along, he was so badly bruised from his fall into the giant's arms. It made him feel so helpless, and as he followed the giant across the auditorium with Amy, his fear began to return. He tried to hold back his tears. He kept seeking the giant with the corner of his eye, waiting to see her next move, waiting for her to turn on him.

She led them to the corridor where they had come in. She pushed the boarding away and the long nails slid out of their solid beds of hard wood. Peter watched in secret horror. He knew what strength was needed to move those nails. Amy slid through the gap, then Peter. Then to his horror, the giant slid after them.

'She's going to help you,' said Amy proudly. Peter almost panicked. The cosy atmosphere in the little room had gone. Was she going to finish him off on the way back? She could do anything – throw him over a rooftop, break him in her hand. And then it would be Amy's turn.

The giant turned and swooped down at him. Peter cried out, backed off. But she had him in her arms and he was lifted up from the ground. She stood with Peter cradled in her arms for a moment, looking at him as if he were a doll. He remembered when he was tiny and his mother held him like this. For a moment she cradled him against her cheek. Then, she bent down and picked Amy up. With the two children cradled in the crooks of her arms, she stepped cautiously out of the shadow and onto the road.

Despite her size, the giant moved like a cat, quickly and smoothly sliding in and out of the shadows. Close up to her, Peter felt calmer. Maybe he sensed something of her true nature from the way she carried him – tenderly, gently, so as not to hurt or jog his injuries. He knew her arms hurt her because she winced and gently re-arranged him from time to time.

Peter gave up. He'd never get away anyway. He was helpless, he had to trust her. He realised properly for the first time – 'She saved me ...' he thought. She had chased him but then she had saved him. From the back of his memory, wiped out before by his panic, he remembered her long form rushing out of the darkness beneath him, the way she had swung him in a circle in her arms to try and slow his fall as gently as she could ...

Peter relaxed in her arms. Why should she kill him now when she could have let him fall and die all on his own? She'd saved his life ...

They sped home. Peter cuddled up against her warmth and watched her face against the dark sky.

The giant woman put him down outside the house. She stood and stared; Peter stared back. Then a car turned into their road. She turned her head, took a few strides away and was gone, hiding briefly by the side of a house until the car passed. Amy and Peter crouched behind the hedge. They watched her emerge from the shadows, a shadow herself. She ran swiftly down the road and was gone.

At the back door to the still house Amy turned her anxious face up to him. 'What are we going to tell them?' she begged.

Peter said nothing. It was so unknown. She'd let him go this time but . . . she was inhuman. He ought to go to the police. Why, he had nearly died because of her!

Amy looked up at him. She trusted him. 'I'll think of something,' he said. Amy smiled.

He opened the door. It seemed impossible that their parents had slept through the whole thing. The kitchen clock said four o'clock. They had been gone hours! It seemed incredible, but no one knew. The house was still.

At the bottom of the stairs, Peter paused. 'Amy,' he whispered. They were standing next to a sawn-off log in the hallway – his parents used it to sit on when they were on the telephone. 'Help me upstairs with it,' he begged.

Between the two of them they managed to haul the heavy lump of wood up the stairs without making too much noise. Then, he told Amy to go to bed. She paused, unsure of him. Then she reached up and hugged him fiercely, binding him to her. Peter waited until she was in her room, listened for the sound of her crawling into bed. Then he pushed the lump of wood downstairs with his foot.

It pounded and banged and thudded like thunder

in the sleeping house, all the way to the bottom. Peter slid after it, trying not to use his back which hurt him most of all. He heard his dad yelling, 'What . . .!' and his mother wake up with a small cry. At the bottom he hurriedly pushed the log back into place.

The only dodgy thing was sounding as if he'd only just hurt himself. He opened his mouth to yell, feeling that it was impossible, they'd know he was acting. But funnily enough, once he began to cry his voice began to shake and the cries welled up from deep inside. It was not the pain of his injuries, but the pain of his fright – the terror from the darkness. But his parents wouldn't know that. He was crying for real.

Chapter 6

There were no bones broken, but Peter's back was bruised black.

He had a few days off school. He had plenty of time to lie there staring at the ceiling thinking about it.

How could such a thing be true? He dreamt one night that it was nothing but a dream; he would have believed it really was a dream and that he'd sleepwalked and fallen downstairs if it wasn't for Amy. She came back from school, walked into his room and whispered, 'Now you know too . . .' It scared the life out of him.

On the evening of the second day Peter was allowed to go out for a walk. He and Amy walked across the meadows to see the old tree. Amy showed him the cage of roots that had been ripped and torn and behind it, the form of the giant woman. Now the earth had collapsed and there was nothing but a long, shapeless hollow among the roots.

Peter climbed painfully down into the crater and began digging with a stick. Although the sun was shining brightly it never reached inside the crater. It was a dungeon. Peter touched the clammy soil gingerly. He found nothing there. But when he started on the disc of earth the tree had torn from the ground he soon turned up a mass of thick reddish-black strands, tangled into a clot.

'Her hair. She tore it out when she escaped,' explained Amy.

Peter flung it away in disgust. He carried on digging in the clods of earth that had fallen from the roots above until at last his fingers found something hard and sharp. Peter dug it out with his hand. At first he thought it was just a stone. But he had seen such stones in a book before now.

'It's an arrowhead,' he said in surprise. You never found such things, you only heard about them. No one had seen this one for thousands of years.

Excitedly he began to dig some more. Amy helped. Together the children uncovered three more arrowheads. Long ago, a man had skilfully chipped away at a rough flint to form these perfect, deadly shapes. He had killed with them, perhaps. They were still sharp enough to cut your finger.

The children climbed out and sat in the sunlight. Peter was thrilled. He was making discoveries. Amy sat by his side and looked anxiously at the little things.

'She comes from the Stone Age,' said Peter. 'Before they even used metal. There were mammoths,' he said, half closing his eyes and recalling his books. 'Cave bears.'

And giants.

'She was wounded,' said Amy firmly.

Peter was about to scoff, but he remembered how Amy knew things. He looked anxiously at her and nodded. 'They hunted her,' he explained. 'She must

73

have been from a different tribe. Maybe they were scared of her – like I was.'

He looked at the relics in his hand. What had happened, so long ago? 'She's from the Stone Age,' he said to himself. He was thrilled. It was a mystery and he was opening it up.

'We want to go on a picnic,' explained Amy.

Outside the sun was shining on the wreckage from the storm. By the sides of the roads were piles of logs, the sawn-up remains of the fallen trees. In the fields they still lay untouched. Some had wilted but most had some roots still in the ground and lived on. A little breeze was moving in the leaves. The land was recovering. Tiny new seedlings were covering the bare earth ripped up around the fallen trees' roots. The air was warm. It was the perfect day for a picnic.

Mrs Lee looked suspiciously at Peter.

'Where to?'

'Riddler's Wood,' he said.

Mrs Lee looked away and scowled. 'Too far,' she said shortly. Riddler's Wood was beyond the meadows – well beyond Amy's range. She turned to end the conversation.

'Sorry, Amy,' said Peter. 'You'll have to stay here . . .'

Amy wailed, 'Mum!'

'Take her to the meadows. What's wrong with the meadows?' demanded Mrs Lee.

'Nothing,' explained Peter. 'Except that I'm going

74

to Riddler's Wood. Amy wants to come. But I don't mind . . .'

'Why can't you be more co-operative with your sister?'

'You're the one who's not letting her go.'

Peter always had an answer. Mrs Lee started shouting then, but Amy was wailing. 'Please, Mum, please, Mum . . . don't be mean . . .'

'I'm not being mean!' howled Mrs Lee. 'He is!'

Peter and Amy had many fights and it often seemed to their mother that Peter spent half his time bullying his little sister. And yet they were good friends. Mary Lee would have fought tooth and nail with Peter, who was more trouble than ten Amys. But he just stood and waited while she argued it out with Amy. Mrs Lee found it very hard to refuse her daughter anything. Amy won hands down.

Once she'd accepted the idea, Mrs Lee was enthusiastic. She'd have the morning to herself. Peter, despite everything, was quite responsible and it was all countryside, there were no roads. She started to look for treats and lectured Peter on how to take care of his sister while she packed the picnic.

'I can look after her all right,' he insisted.

She glared. 'I've seen your looking after before now.'

She began to lose her nerve as she stood in the garden waving them goodbye. Riddler's Wood was miles off!

'Don't talk to any strangers!'

'Of course not!'

'If you get fed up and walk off without her, you'll be grounded for a month!' she blustered.

'Don't be silly!'

Mrs Lee ground her teeth in rage, but it was too late to order them back. The fuss Amy would make . . . Trust Peter to start cheeking her as soon as he was on his way . . .

The two children walked across the short, thick grass to the river and threaded their way along it until they were out of sight of the house. Then they cut across country on the footpath that led them into town.

As they crossed the fields Peter ran ahead and laughed. But when they left the grass and walked up a narrow alley that led them onto the streets, he became quiet. Now they were going back to the dark, back to the creature that lived in the dark. The monster.

Amy skipped and sang. She was more at ease than ever now. Before she had carried the secret alone. She'd had to lie and plot. Now all that was up to Peter. She had no duties anymore. She had only to love her friend.

On the big road they held hands. They were nervous someone who knew them would see them. There was no hiding place, they had to brazen it out. The cinema waited for them, like a blinded giant itself with its windows boarded-up and closed. The litter seemed to gather around it. They hung about outside till the way was clear. It wasn't a busy part of town. Then they swiftly ran down past the rubbish and the heaps of binbags.

The board was already loose when they arrived. Peter felt a shiver of fear as he looked at the gap into darkness. He could smell her, rich and horsy and spicy. He thought he heard her breath. He glanced back – he could still run for it. But Amy was already in. She was never alone in the dark anymore. Peter pushed his shoulder into the gap and squeezed through after her. The huge dark shape was waiting.

Inside her hideaway behind the cinema screen there were candles burning. Peter sat down and watched awkwardly. Amy at once climbed up onto Giant's lap and hugged and stroked her. Giant stroked her back. Peter felt she was watching him with the corner of her eye. She understood Amy but he was as strange to her as she was to him. He didn't belong.

He opened his bag. 'We brought you some apples,' he said. He held one out to her.

Giant turned to look at him. He watched her great head turning – like a horse turning to look intelligently at him. Her huge eyes watched him closely, suspiciously. She reached out and took the apple and laid it by her side. She nodded.

'We brought you some other things . . .' Nervously he emptied his bag – bread, butter, candles, fruit, chocolate. He looked up at her. 'I won't tell . . . I won't do anything that you don't want,' he said earnestly. If only he could get through to her, make her understand, like she understood Amy.

She leaned forward towards him. Peter gasped in fright but he sat still. She put her arm around him . . . and kissed him.

Peter put his arms around her. She was so warm. He stroked her long hair. It was like a horse's mane. She smelt sweet close up.

'We'll help,' he said. Giant leaned back, Peter touched the place where she'd kissed him. She was tender and gentle. He didn't know how but she was helpless and lost.

'We'll help,' he said again.

He began to take out some other things he had brought. The four arrowheads.

As she watched him take the sharp little things out and hold them in the palm of his hand, Amy felt her heart jump; Giant knew these. Peter was watching Giant closely but he would have been better watching Amy. In her face, not in Giant's still face, the giant's feelings showed.

'Wounded,' said Amy. Giant turned and touched her back. They looked but there were no scars.

'Maybe she healed up in the ground,' said Peter. Amy shrugged.

Peter opened a book. 'Mammoth,' he said, pointing to a picture. 'Did you see one of those? Did she see one of those?' he begged Amy.

Amy shrugged. 'I don't know,' she said scornfully. It wasn't like that between them. She didn't know

78

about things . . .

'Look . . .' Giant followed his finger with a steady gaze. 'Woolly rhinoceros. Do you know it? Hyena . . .'

'You don't get hyenas over here,' scoffed Amy.

'But you did then – when she was alive. They lived all round here. They find the bones in caves . . . Look! Sabre-toothed cat.'

Giant shook her head. Peter looked so disappointed that she seized her lips in her hands and pushed the corners up, into a smile.

Peter laughed and nodded.

Amy began to laugh too. 'Now do a sad face,' she ordered. She pulled a sad face to show her. Giant tried, but it didn't work out somehow.

'No – that's surprised!' exclaimed Amy. She clambered over and began to push the big still face about with her fingers. 'You have to turn your mouth down – there! Sad face . . .'

Peter howled with laughter. It still wasn't right. The eyebrows were all wrong. He jumped over and helped, pulling her eyebrows together. 'That's sad,' he said. But it still wasn't right.

'Now do angry,' said Amy. And she pulled her little round face into a furious scowl

They did all the faces – happy, sad, angry, frightened, twisting and pulling her face this way and that. Giant sat patiently and did her best, but she just didn't have the muscles and the faces just fell away when they let go. It was so funny. They were both howling with laughter. Amy found a mirror

and held it up so Giant could see and then her
shoulders began to shake. Her stomach went up
and down and she made a fluting, whistling noise.
Her face remained as still as a mask and they
laughed louder than ever.

When it was all over and everyone could sit still
again, Giant took the book up from the floor and
began to leaf through it.

'She won't know how to read,' explained Peter
to Amy. Amy pulled a face. Peter was so keen to
tell her things but she was the one who knew, really.

'She's a primitive,' he went on. 'She doesn't know
very much I expect. Maybe we can teach her – I
wonder if she can make arrowheads . . .'

The woman leaned over to him. She was pointing
at a picture of a bear. Peter nodded. 'Bear,' he said.

Giant pointed at the picture. 'Wear,' she said.

Amy scowled. 'You can talk,' she said in a hurt
voice.

It hadn't been necessary with Amy. But with
Peter, who as far as the giant was concerned was
blind in a kind of way, the words were worth trying.
She found it difficult to get her mouth around them,
but she tried for his sake.

Peter beamed. He was teaching her! He was finding out more.

Suddenly she put down the book. She got up and
left the room. They heard her rummaging about.
She came back with some paint pots. During the
long hours on her own she had wandered about in
the darkness, exploring with the torch and the cand-

les Amy had brought her. She had found these pots of paint in a cupboard, which had been left over from the last time the foyer had been decorated.

She led Peter and Amy into the auditorium by the big screen. Carefully she levered the tops off with a piece of metal, dipped her brush in the green paint and began to make a picture.

Giant drew a bear. She wasn't terribly good at drawing, but it was definitely a bear. In case they weren't sure she pointed to the picture in the book, and said, 'Wear,' again.

'See!' Peter was delighted with himself. 'I told you she was Stone Age. She's seen them – cave bears!'

Amy sat down on the edge of the screen and watched. She wasn't sure what Peter was doing, but she liked watching Giant draw. She was happy because they were friends.

Peter pointed to a picture of cavemen in the book. They were shaggy and hairy and wrapped in skins. He held it up. Giant nodded, and began to paint.

Peter was excited. He would be the first one to know what cavemen really looked like. She'd seen them. She was one! But in the end he was disappointed. The drawings were really rather poor – you couldn't tell anything about what they'd really looked like from these.

She drew two. One of them was holding a bow and arrows.

Peter pointed at her and then at the cavemen.

'You,' he said. 'Giant . . .' and he pointed again at the picture. He wanted to tell her that she was one of them, one of the cavemen she'd painted.

But she understood something else. She began to paint again – this time, herself. She was still a giant; she had been a giant to the cavemen, too. She was naked. She was running away from the men. In her back were arrows.

'She was being hunted,' jabbered Peter to Amy excitedly.

'I said,' replied Amy scornfully. But Peter was too excited to care.

He pointed at her again. She watched him closely. 'Two giants,' he said, pointing to the screen. She shook her head. She didn't understand.

Peter thought she came from a tribe who had died out. He wanted her to draw her own type.

He tried again. He pointed to himself. 'One child,' he said. He held out one finger. Then he turned to Amy. 'Two children,' he said, holding two fingers up. Then, to the giant. 'One giant . . .' holding up one finger. Then, holding up two, 'Two giants!' And he pointed to the screen.

Now she understood. It was wonderful that he could make her understand him. But she looked sad. She held out two fingers and shook her head. She held out one finger and nodded. 'Un,' she said. Peter frowned and shook his head. She tried again.

'Un . . . ant . . .'

'One giant,' said Amy suddenly. She came over to stroke her friend. It was sad. Giant was all alone.

There was only one of her.

'That's impossible,' said Peter. He tried again and again to get her to draw her tribe, but Giant refused to paint anything but herself.

Chapter 7

No creature came from nowhere. No creature was only one. Had she just grown like a plant in the roots of the oak tree? Or perhaps she came from a time before even the Stone Age, an earlier time ... before people?

Peter was certain she was a primitive. She didn't do anything, she just sat there. She knew so little. She was so slow at learning the words he tried to teach her. She still couldn't even pronounce his name. Her drawings were like children's drawings. He got more books from the library and from school. The Stone Age, he learned, went on for thousands and thousands of years. But no one had ever heard of people so tall.

'She must be an extinct type,' he told Amy. Amy shrugged. It meant nothing to her. Giant came out of the ground, out of the past. And now she was here with them.

Amy said she was waiting. But what for? Maybe they had magic in those days and it had gone wrong while she waited under the ground and she didn't know it. Peter was sure that whatever it was she was waiting for, it had happened hundreds or thousands of years ago and she had missed it in her sleep.

'She must be a cave dweller,' he told Amy. 'Look

at how she lives in that horrible cinema . . . all dark. It must be like home to her.'

'She's hiding,' explained Amy patiently. She wondered why her brother, who usually knew so much more than she did, was so slow with Giant. Amy did not know who Giant was or what she was waiting for. But she knew that all the things she loved were outside, in the light.

One thing Peter was sure of; sooner or later, the giant would be found out. It wasn't possible to hide such a great, strange creature in the middle of a town for long. People would get to hear of it. At first they wouldn't believe but then they'd come and see and they'd take her away. It would be in all the papers. It would be on TV! People would want to speak to him and ask him what the giant was like.

Peter wanted to find out as much as he could about her. He wanted to know more about her than anyone. But although he quizzed her and Amy, although he tried to teach her to speak, although he showed her books and made her paint, he could not find out what she was, or where she came from, or what it was she was waiting for.

It was a month since Peter had followed Amy through the night to the old cinema. They had seen Giant three more times since then. It was difficult. Peter was surprised that they'd got away with it for so long. Every day he waited to hear the news that something strange was going on at the old Roxy. Barricades and roadblocks would be put up, the police would come, the TV cameras. Then the secret would be out and he could speak. But so far nothing had happened. The cinema stood ignored and unused. His father said it would be turned into a carpet warehouse one day but that wouldn't be for months or years.

One night Peter lay in bed unable to sleep, staring out of his curtains at the shadows over the garden in front of the house. He thought of Giant sitting in her dark place. What was she doing now? What did she think, when she was alone? Did she think at all? Or just feel, like an animal? He wondered if there were other giants outside in the night. Perhaps she was waiting for them. Perhaps they lived spread out all around the world, living in old churches and cinemas and deserted buildings. Or they slept under the earth and were waking up, one by one . . .

Weeks had gone by and he had found out nothing new. Peter was getting angry. He was sure she knew what he wanted to know. She was just keeping it from him.

After tossing and turning for a long time, Peter got out of bed. He stood for a while on the carpet in his bare feet, watching the darkness outside his room as if it could tell him something. Tonight, the sense of the strangeness of it all was very strong in him. He left the room, paused in the corridor and for some reason – there was no noise or anything – he opened the door to Amy's room. He stared at the bed for a second until he realised with a thrill what was wrong. Amy wasn't there.

He knew at once she was with Giant. He was angry and jealous. It was dangerous to go through the town on her own . . . both for her and for Giant. It was selfish. They couldn't see her very often. Amy had stolen a chance from him.

Peter looked out of the window. He would have gone after her but he had no idea how long she'd been gone. It had never occurred to him to go on his own to Giant. He would have been too scared. Yet Amy had done it. For a second he considered going to tell his parents that Amy was missing . . . it would serve her right. But he wasn't ready to do that.

Sulkily he sat down in the chair by her bed. He pulled a blanket from the bed over him. He'd wait. There was no chance of sleeping now, anyway.

He didn't have to wait long.

There was a noise at the window. The window was on the first floor . . . it made him jump out of his chair. He heard the giant snuffing the air. Then Amy appeared on the window-sill.

Peter showed himself at the window. He saw the still, big face looking back up at him.

Amy squeaked in surprise. They all looked guiltily at each other for a second. Then Amy climbed down to the floor.

'I'm sorry,' she said. Then she added, 'We just wanted to be on our own . . .'

Poor Amy could not explain. She had so many feelings in her that came from Giant – longing, fear, impatience. But most often, most of all, she felt

Giant's loneliness. Giant was so far from her time, so far from her place. No one had ever been as alone as she was. Amy was an opening into her heart and she loved the little girl for it.

'She took you outside,' said Peter. 'She shouldn't go outside.'

Amy pulled a face, but she said nothing. On the other side of the window, in the night, Giant leaned with her back to the wall and waited.

'Do you do it often?' said Peter. He felt almost like crying. It was so unfair!

'Not often,' said Amy. 'A few times. But . . .' But she couldn't explain. She didn't understand herself why it was important for Giant to be with her sometimes . . . without Peter. Giant had no way of knowing her brother.

Outside the window Giant turned and held her hands up. She rested them on the sill. Amy nudged Peter.

'Go on,' she said. 'It's your turn.'

'I don't want to,' said Peter automatically, in a sulky voice. But he took a half step towards the window.

'Go on . . .' urged Amy. Peter took another couple of steps; the hands beckoned. Peter climbed up onto the window-sill and sat there. He still felt furious. Giant watched him closely. Then she reached up.

She seized him round the waist. He held his breath. He had wanted this but he didn't trust her, either. She could dash him to the ground now! Was it a trick? She lifted him onto her hip and walked in long easy strides behind the house.

Peter held on tight and tried not to let his face show what he felt – fear, excitement and sulkiness all together. He felt like a great, ugly baby as she carried him along. She walked behind the house and over the garden. She stepped over the hedge at the end as if it were merely a step. Then she began to run.

It was fast – so fast! The dark hedges and fields like shadows whipped past him. He gulped at the air in his throat. He could hear her feet landing in thuds in the grass but it seemed to him that they were flying and her footsteps were the pounding of wings in the air.

Across the fields they flew. Peter forgot his fear and his anger and held on. He began to cry out in a shrill voice, but she hushed him. He tried to keep quiet then, but he had to bite his lips as the world whizzed past in darkness.

Suddenly she grasped his waist, lifted him up and whirled him round and round and round. The whole world swam. He began to scream so she stopped, but it was just excitement.

Then she stood still and looked down into his face to see if she had done the right thing.

Peter was thrilled. 'Thank you . . . thank you . . .!' he gasped. It was like flying. On an impulse he leaned forward and hugged her and then pulled back to see her reaction.

Giant's still, unknowable face stared back at him. Amy would have known what she felt. She was anxious – was this what the boy wanted? Had she pleased him? What did hugging mean? But Peter was closed to her. He saw only her face as still as a machine.

His excitement fizzled out inside him and he again felt awkward, uncomfortable – at risk.

He leaned back from her. 'Thank you,' he said again, nervously.

Giant nodded and began to walk back. They walked some way in silence. It was bad between them again – it had to be bad because there was no way they could share their feelings. But she wanted to show him she meant well. She wanted to share something with him. She stopped walking.

Peter looked nervously at her. Giant pointed up to the sky. Peter followed her finger. It was a dark sky, a few clouds, some stars moving in and out of sight. The orange lights of the town cast an ugly light onto the clouds.

'The sky?' he asked.

Giant pointed at the ground. She scuffed at it with her heel, made a hole. Then she pointed at herself. She glanced at Peter.

'You?' he said uncertainly. He had no idea what she wanted.

Giant shook her head furiously and pointed up again.

Above him a cloud rolled by. The stars moved in and out of its shadow. Giant stamped her foot impatiently. She pointed at herself, and again up, to the stars.

Up to the stars . . .

Then he realised. It was simple! She didn't come from the ground at all . . .

'You . . .' he cried. He seized her around the neck and pointed. 'From the stars? The stars?'

Giant nodded. She looked at him carefully and said, 'Stars . . .'

Not from the ground at all. From up there, up there . . .

'From another planet!' cried Peter. Giant lifted her hand to her mouth and formed a smile.

They stood in the cow field and looked up to where the stars shone.

Chapter 8

Not from the past at all – from the future. Peter had made a great discovery. She trusted him, she was telling him. He loved her for it. But his curiosity was burning hotter than ever.

The woman showed him more. Using the paint she had found in the cinema, she began to paint pictures – landscapes of tall people and long trees and unfamiliar plants. Strange birds with people on their backs. Creatures that looked like llamas or giraffes. Tall people doing things he could never understand. Her world – the world she had left behind.

Somewhere around one of the stars shining above was a planet not so very different from this one, where people lived. Some of them left their home and flew in between the stars and visited the earth . . .

It all fell together. She was waiting. One day very soon, her ship would come to take her away. She had only to wait and remain undiscovered, and she would get back to her home and her own kind.

The mystery was solved.

But there were other mysteries Peter could not unravel. Was it her storm that blew down the trees and tore her out of the ground? Was she lost, left behind, abandoned, or was there a purpose to her long wait? What had she to do with Amy and himself, and why had she been buried in the earth, living and unliving at the same time?

He tried to ask these questions. But the words of earth were so strange to her lips and she could not talk – just one or two simple words. There was no sign she understood what he said.

One thing he did discover – it would happen soon. Giant did not understand the earth calendar, or the phases of the moon. But she had an idea of the seasons. She drew a picture of a tree with leaves falling from it. Autumn. At the end of the summer, she would go.

Amy pulled a face. She would be sad to lose her friend. Peter made a face too and pretended he was unhappy for the same reason. But his disappointment was for another reason. If all went well Giant would escape unseen, unheard. There would be no television cameras, no newspaper pictures, no fame, no questions. Peter would have seen the most wonderful thing in the world and no one would ever know.

And that was a pity.

Peter often imagined the landing – Giant walking up to the ship, into it . . . He and Amy would be there of course to wave goodbye and perhaps they would be given some souvenir or reward, something they could show people afterwards. More than anything, Peter wanted them to leave behind some proof that he could show people. He felt he would die if he had to keep this wonderful adventure a secret all his life.

Peter wanted to know so much – what the star-ships were like, how they were powered, where they travelled. He wanted to know where she was from. When she was back with her own people and he was able to talk about it, he wanted to look up and see the star she had gone to. He found a map of the stars in an astronomy book at home and asked Giant to show him which one was hers.

She couldn't do it. He got Amy to help him, but Amy wasn't even sure that Giant knew what a star map was. It was so stupid! He was annoyed. She was a traveller between the stars but she didn't even know which one she came from.

Peter had a plan. Giant did not understand the map. But if he took her outside on another starry night, surely she would be able to point to her star in the sky.

One day after school, he told his parents he was going to visit a friend of his who lived a few streets away. He had to be back for tea, but that gave him plenty of time.

He left quietly by the front, so that Amy, who was playing in her room at the back, wouldn't see him go. Today, for the first time, he was going to see Giant on his own.

It was so hard to take Amy along. No one both-ered about a ten-year-old out on his own, but they noticed Amy. Then they had to get permission from their mother, and there was the danger of Amy being seen where she wasn't supposed to be . . .

Besides, Amy and the giant got so wrapped up in each other. He had important questions to ask. He'd get more out of her if Amy wasn't around to mess things up.

Peter ran swiftly down the road, past the houses, past the scattered shops and the zebra crossing towards the old cinema. It was easy on his own!

It was drizzling. The litter lay in soggy heaps around the foot of the big old building. There weren't many people out; no one spotted him as he dashed down the little side alley, hid a moment among the boxes, and then crept up to knock on the loose hoarding.

He was worried she wouldn't open up for him, or that she wouldn't know who it was. He waited until he thought she was near and called softly. The board began to move away to make a gap for him to get in. It was all right! He slipped inside. Giant pushed the board closed again and watched him standing on the grubby carpet, trying to smile and get his breath back at the same time. Then she silently turned and led the way in.

It felt . . . dangerous. He hated the way her face kept so still. Amy somehow made it safe. He wanted to get through to her that she should come round to his window and pick him up again. He wanted to feel that rush of air again, watch the night rushing quietly past him. He wanted her to show him her star in the sky. She would share her secrets with him alone, when Amy was asleep in bed.

He was standing in the small room watching her

as she lit candles when he noticed she was limping.

He pointed at her leg. Giant pulled a face.

Peter had given her pencils and paper so that she could draw things for him, to show him what she meant. Now she took them and made a little sketch. A small, fierce animal. Her drawing was awful; it was a while before Peter worked out that it was a dog.

'You've been bitten,' he said. 'You went outside and a dog got you . . .'

He made a barking noise and bit with his teeth. Giant nodded and lifted her skirt to show him her ankle. It was a bad bite. It was still bleeding slightly.

'You shouldn't go out!' Peter scolded. Then he had a thought. 'Was there anyone there?' He began to mime – he was getting good at it by this time – a man with the dog.

The woman picked up the paper and drew again. Yes – a man with the dog. She looked at him and pointed to herself. She looked scared, like a frightened little girl.

She had been seen! Peter felt a thrill of excitement go through him. If she got caught and it was nothing to do with him, how perfect it would be! He would be able to tell everyone after all.

He began to mime again – himself, the outside, the stars. She didn't understand at first, but when she got it she shook her head firmly. Not now she had been seen. It was just too dangerous.

Peter scowled. This wasn't what he wanted at all. It was unfair. It wasn't his fault she had gone out and got caught. He was doing so much for her – bringing her food, coming to talk to her. He was even going to let her go and never tell a soul he had met her. And she wasn't even willing to take him out one more time!

He began to mime again. He didn't hide his anger. She owed him. It was stupid. No one would see them if they were careful. And even if they were seen, who'd believe it? No one believed in giants in this day and age.

Giant stared carefully at him with her unknowable eyes. She shook her head again.

Peter was furious. She owed him! As he stared at her, he had a sense that big though she was, she was in his power. He could control her. He could decide whether or not she ever saw her own sun shining in the sky again.

'You take me,' said Peter, 'or I'll tell.'

There was a horrible moment. She watched him. Peter glanced around him as if Amy were hiding in the shadows, listening. Giant didn't take her eyes off him. He had no idea if she understood him or not.

She shook her head. The moment passed. Peter thought she hadn't understood. He was glad. He hadn't meant it. He'd been angry.

He looked at his feet and shuffled. 'Okay,' he said. 'I'd better be going home now.'

Giant led him down the aisle and out to the corridor. She pushed open the board for him. Peter slipped out, glad to be in the fresh air. He was glad she hadn't understood. He hadn't meant it, not really . . .

Later, as he lay in bed, Peter felt worse than ever about it. He really hoped she hadn't understood – it would be horrible if she'd understood. He kept thinking about Amy. He hadn't seen much of his sister that evening but she'd been very quiet at teatime. His mother had noticed and asked her if anything was wrong. At the time Peter hadn't thought anything of it but now, he wondered. Amy always knew what Giant was thinking. Did she know what had passed between her and him?

Peter tossed and turned and felt worse and worse. In the end he promised himself that he'd tell Amy all about it first thing in the morning. She'd explain – she'd understand and tell Giant he hadn't really meant it. He was on her side. Of course he'd never give her away – he was just angry. He'd do anything he could to help.

That thought helped him to get to sleep.

When he awoke the next morning it was in his mind first thing.

He felt different now. He didn't really want to go and tell his little sister what he'd done. Maybe it didn't matter after all. He went through to see her anyway but when he opened the door and looked at the bed, Amy wasn't there.

Chapter 9

He didn't give up hope straight away. But he knew. He ran to his room to pull on some clothes and went downstairs. He was in a hurry, he was too noisy. His father called after him as he ran up the drive but he didn't turn round.

Peter was in such a panic already that he hardly bothered to hide himself. Startled faces followed him on the street. A neighbour called his name. Peter shouted back, trying to sound cheerful. He ran along onto the main road and towards the old Roxy.

Down the alley. The usual mess of cardboard boxes, paper, packing boxes and old vegetables from the nearby shops. It was cool and damp. At the end of it, the loose board hung off the wall.

It was open. The cinema no longer had anything to hide. Peter went in anyway. He wouldn't believe it until he had to.

Inside it was as dark as ever. He'd been foolish not to bring a torch. He was even more scared now that it really was empty; the dark was a worse monster than Giant. Or was she waiting in there? Did she hate him now? He called, 'Amy? Amy, please . . .!' There was no answer. He didn't expect one. He knew. He'd known as soon as he saw the empty bed. Giant had gone and Amy had gone with her.

Peter began to snivel as he made his way back out. It was so unfair! He'd only said that one thing wrong, he had only let that one bad thought cross his mind. He hadn't even meant it. And now he had this on his shoulders.

When he reached the loose board he stopped and blinked at the daylight. He wiped his nose on his sleeve. Giants, aliens, creatures from space – it all seemed impossible out here. The deserted cinema was a world of strange dreams. Inside were the paintings on the screen of her world, of the alien people and their plants and animals. Peter remembered the storm. It was Giant's storm. People had died in it. Now she had run off with Amy and it was his fault.

He began to run home, but he stopped as he neared his house and walked. He began to cry. What would he say to his parents? How could he tell them? What could he say?

Peter got into the kitchen and went to the fridge for juice. His dad was there making tea.

'Where've you been?' he asked sleepily.

Peter fumbled with the door of the fridge. 'Out for a walk.' His dad looked curiously at him.

Minutes passed.

'Amy?' called his mother from upstairs. She'd just discovered the empty bed.

Peter's dad glanced at Peter and stuck his head into the living room for a look. 'She's not downstairs,' he called.

'She's not up here,' called his mother. Peter's dad glanced at Peter. Peter shook his head.

They weren't that worried, not yet. In the past few weeks Amy had gone out into the meadows in the mornings more than once. To his disgust Peter was made to go out and look for her.

'But she won't be there!' he insisted angrily.

'What makes you so sure?' asked his mother. She was watching him suspiciously. He'd been up early, too. What did he know? He could see the suspicion behind her eyes. She was angry with him already and she knew nothing! Peter shrugged and walked out of the back door and down the garden.

He wandered up and down the meadow with a poisoned heart. He should have told them at once. Then it would be over with already but now he had to go back and tell them.

But tell them what? That there was a big bad giant?

Peter stood and watched the muddy brown water flow past. He turned and walked back home. He'd tell them now. He climbed over the stile and walked up the garden. He felt like a monster coming to the house. His father was out in the streets looking for her. He found his mother in the kitchen and started to tell her at once.

Then it was the police.

It was awful. It kept going on and on. First his parents. His mother screaming at him. Then a policeman asking him questions. Every time his mother looked at him he felt something die inside him, because she was right, the things she was thinking. He should have known better. Running off to see strangers in the middle of the night! He was the eldest. What had he done to Amy?

After that he had to go to the police station and there was a woman and a tape recorder.

She was sweet and polite and listened carefully to him talking about the storm, the woman in the earth, the four arrowheads. She had the same expression when he told her about the giant in the cinema, how she lifted them in and out of the window, how she spoke to Amy with her mind.

'Do you believe me?' he begged her when it was over, the third time he had told his story in a few hours.

The policewoman smiled her careful smile. 'Everything you've told me is true, I'm sure,' she said. Peter nodded desperately. 'Only,' she added, '. . . only I don't believe in giants.' She smiled again. This time her smile was a little bit grim.

'Then what was she?' Peter begged.

'A woman,' she said. She glanced at Peter curiously, to watch this news sink in.

'She was tall . . .' began Peter.

'Yes, a very tall woman. It should make her easier to find.' The policewoman smiled, sweet again.

'But what about her face?' demanded Peter.

She frowned. 'Yes, that is odd. The only thing I can think is that she was wearing a mask.' She glanced uneasily at him as she packed up the tape-machine. Afterwards she took him for a drink in the canteen. The policemen nodded and smiled familiarly and tried to chat with him but Peter was far away.

He was thinking how often they had asked him if he'd seen her in the light, and he never had, not once. Had her face just seemed that way, in the dark?

What sort of person would wear a mask like that?

Perhaps she was mad.

What did a mad woman want with his sister?

In the police car on the way back the memories came – memories of other little girls and boys who had disappeared with strangers. Sometimes they came back. Sometimes they never did. Sometimes they were missing for days or weeks or months. Sometimes they were found in shallow graves in the woods and waste places.

That evening Amy was on the television. She had been abducted by a tall woman with torn black hair. The woman was last seen wearing clothes made from an old curtain. She was mentally disturbed. She was potentially dangerous and should not be approached.

Peter's mother, sitting on the sofa, fell over sideways onto his father and wept. Peter sat very still and held onto his chair. They didn't look at him but he knew what they were thinking. They were right. It was all his fault.

He had betrayed everyone.

Chapter 10

There was a small wood with a footpath that curled round inside it. Beyond was a field with long grass, docks, nettles and willow herb growing tall. In the field was an old church.

The church had not been empty long. The roof was still on. Only a few years ago there had still been services there, but so few people came. It was far from any villages. Now it was slowly falling down.

Amy and Giant were hiding inside.

Giant found the words hard to say but she was quick to learn. Her mouth wasn't made for talk, but she had understood every word Peter said. Amy didn't really believe it was so serious. Peter might have threatened but he'd never really give her away. She tried to get this across but Giant didn't seem to understand. All she knew was she was threatened and she had to go on the run. Amy would never let her go alone.

Giant carried her in her arms as she made her way past the still hedges and the sleeping houses. Soon Amy slept. Giant ran softly, so as not to wake the little one. Sometimes she wept as she ran.

She was so close. Another week or so and the time would be right. After so long, after so much trying and hiding and waiting, she mustn't get caught now. She'd thought she was safe but there was no end to the danger and the hiding from it. She had to hide better, deeper, further away . . .

They had passed several barns early on but Amy didn't like them. They looked good to Giant – empty, a long way from houses. She didn't realise that the farmers could come by any time. But when they came to the church Amy was asleep. Giant was tired. She crept into the building.

It was damper and colder than the cinema. There were no carpets or seats. The floor was cold stone. But it felt still and safe. She lay down on the stones with Amy still wrapped in the folds of her curtain robes, and went to sleep at once.

When she woke up again Amy was standing in the door looking out at the pale light.

'This isn't a good place to hide,' said Amy.

Giant looked around. It was light. Sunlight was pouring in through the holes in the roof, through the arched door and windows, breaking up the darkness.

It was beautiful.

Every day in the cinema she had dreamed of the sun. On this still, beautiful morning in late summer, it was difficult to believe that the sun was dangerous.

She tried to smile for Amy. The little girl stood watching her seriously. She was scared. Giant knew she ought to be scared, too. But how could she be scared when the world was full of warming? She could smell the sun, the dew drying on the grass, the little lives in the bushes and plants, the leaves changing colour.

Giant got up and walked to a window and put her head out. She snuffed the air. It was all so beautiful. She felt that she would rather be caught than hide away from the sun another day.

She turned to Amy and waved her hand out of the window. She wanted the girl to share her feelings.

'I know,' said Amy. 'But this is a bad place to hide.'

Giant walked round to the door. She breathed. She put her hand outside. She felt the air on her hand. She left the church.

There were birds singing. She felt all the little movements in the grass and bushes. There were tiny black and red berries on the bushes that smelt of sugar and wine. Something flew by; it was a complete surprise, it shocked her. It was black and red. It landed on the bushes and fanned its wings. She crept up to watch. It was a jewel. It smelt of oranges and electricity and dust.

The butterfly – it was a red admiral – flew off and it surprised her so much she cried out. She loved it; she would never hurt it but she couldn't bear to lose it. She began to chase after it, trying to catch it with swooping motions of her hand. But she was scared of touching it. It flew fast, although it seemed to be made of paper. She had to run to keep up with it. She thought she had never seen anything so surprising and wonderful in her life.

'Come back!' Amy was terrified – of Giant getting

lost, of being left on her own. Her friend seemed to have forgotten everything. She was running off into the bushes and trees, out of sight.

Amy ran after her but she was gone already. She had gone! Left her? But she would be helpless on her own . . .

Amy was scared to call in case she attracted attention. She started to wander amongst the trees and bushes. She felt tears gathering behind her eyes.

'Ba-ha!'

Amy shrieked and jumped. But it was Giant – running from behind a tree to startle and tease her!

Amy was cross only for a second. They were having fun – they could play. It had never occurred to her that they could play. She shouted and ran for her, but Giant ran into the bushes and hid again. Amy ran shrieking round the bushes and Giant roared like a tiger, and caught her and carried her on her back like a horse, and then disappeared again . . .

The game went on for half an hour. At last Amy stopped and started to eat the blackberries off the bushes. Neither of them had eaten anything since the day before. Giant crept up and tried the berries. They were good, but so tiny. They were both ravenous. She sat by Amy and they began to gobble the sweet black berries as fast as they could. It was so good. She nibbled the ends of the brambles where the berries grew. They tasted good too. Giant began to browse, biting the whole cluster of berries off in one mouthful and munching it all down, stalks, thorns and all.

They were still stuffing when they heard voices. Giant picked Amy up and melted into the bushes.

It was a man and a woman. The man held a stick. They had a small dog with them.

Amy pointed deeper into the bushes. Giant quietly pushed her way through them. She moved as softly as a deer. They found a thick bush and hid inside it, listening as the voices came nearer.

The voices got loud, then they began to move away as the people passed. Amy thought they were all right and smiled up at her friend. But the dog was waiting behind. It sniffed. They heard it at the edges of the bushes. Then it barked.

'Come on, Silas... good boy!' shouted the woman. But the dog ignored her. He pressed forward through the bushes, following Giant's strong, sweet scent.

As he got near, the dog got excited. He started to whine with nerves... he'd never smelt anything like this before. When he got closer he began to quiver and bark furiously.

'Silas! What is it? What is it, boy?'

The people were walking back. The dog was within a metre of them and it was barking hysterically. The man and woman began to press past the bushes. The man began beating at the bushes with his stick.

'Must be something hiding in there...' The man was nervous. He beat hard at the bushes.

Suddenly Giant reached out. She was quick, like

a snake. She caught the dog by the scruff of the neck, shook it, and then flung it with a flick of her wrist. The dog flew through the air like a small furry bird, barking in a surprised note. It landed in a bush with a crash. Then it tucked its tail down and fled like a rabbit.

'Hey . . .!'

'Silas . . .?'

The beating stopped. Giant edged into the bushes. They heard the bushes rustle under her weight.

'Must be a badger . . .' said the man uncertainly. But what badger made dogs fly? The man was puzzled. He thrashed at the bushes again.

But the woman laughed. 'Poor Silas! Did it frighten you?' She turned and ran after him. 'He's such a coward. Silas! Silas . . . here, Silas! Don't be such a wimp . . .' The woman ran off down the path. The man stood by the bushes a moment longer.

'Big badger,' he muttered to himself.

'Come on . . . he'll be miles away, he'll get lost. You know what he's like . . .' called the woman from up the path. The man paused a moment longer, and then turned and ran after her. Amy and Giant listened to their footsteps fading.

'I told you it was a bad place,' said Amy.

They had to stay in the woods all day. They didn't dare travel in daylight. People came from time to time. There were a couple more dogs, but none of them got close.

Mostly it was deadly boring, lying low among the bushes. Giant was scared again. She'd been happy for a little bit but now she was scared again. It was the only way to survive in this strange land.

The worst thing was being hungry. Amy got very bad-tempered and sulky about it in the end and went to lie down away from her friend.

In the afternoon it got very warm. They had been up half the night and they both fell asleep, lying in the leaf mould under the bushes. It was a foolish thing to do.

Noise awoke them. There were people. Four boys. They had come across Amy and Giant lying in the long grass. Giant opened her eyes and there they were. She screamed like a factory whistle.

The boys jumped like kangaroos. They began to yell before they hit the ground and then they were off, running through the trees screaming for their mothers, for their fathers, for anyone. Giant snatched Amy off the ground and ran, charging at the bushes, crashing through them, flattening them until she was scratched and bloody. To Amy's relief she ran away from, not after the boys. At last she flung herself down into a thicket and froze.

Amy lay next to her, feeling the quadruple ba-ba-ba-boom of her heart. When her friend was calm, she got up and dusted her dress down.

'I'm hungry,' she complained.

Giant lay on her side and watched her. There was nothing to be done for now. They could only hide and wait. She shook her head. Amy pouted angrily.

Gradually the day faded. When it was completely dark, Giant picked Amy up, put her on her hip and began to pick her way out of the heathland.

Every day Peter saw the story of his stupidity on the news. How the girl and her stupid brother thought they'd found a giant and hidden her in an old cinema. But the giant was really a mad woman who hid her face in a terrible mask, and had run off with the poor little girl. It was told in newspapers, in magazines, on radio and TV. Amy's picture was everywhere: she was famous.

The story really caught fire. Men and women from the newspapers were hanging around all over the place. They were there on the front lawn in the morning, so that Peter and his dad had to run past them when he went to school. They lurked at the school gates, questioning passers-by or taking photographs through the windows with long-distance lenses. They were still there, crowding round him, shoving microphones and cameras in his face as he came out after school. And they were there again as he ran past the crowd outside his house in the afternoon.

It got so bad that the headmaster asked his parents to keep him off school for a few days, until the fuss died down.

So Peter stayed at home and the photographers tried to get snapshots of him peeking out of the windows. Once, as he peeped out from behind the curtains, a man from up the road walked past and spied him peering out.

'You ought to have more bloody sense, a lad of your age. It'll be your fault if anything happens to her!' he yelled. At once, the newspaper men and women gathered around the man, writing down his words. It would be everywhere the next day. It would be on the telly that very evening.

At home his parents did their best but it was obvious they blamed him. This time, they were right. Peter couldn't understand himself how he had been so stupid. So she had been tall . . . so her face was wrong. How could he be such a baby as to believe in giants! And yet – sometimes on his own when the grown-ups weren't there to tell him what was what, he remembered how very alien she had seemed, how Amy had been able to read her mind. Surely she had been more than just a person . . .

Poor Peter. Against him he had his parents, the police, the newspapers, the TV, the whole world. In the end, he believed them before he believed himself.

The police kept coming round to interview him and to talk to his parents. They searched the cinema, of course, from top to bottom. When they found the drawings she had made on the screen Peter felt a flash of hope. The drawings of another planet! Perhaps it wasn't just his imagination after all.

'They were very bad drawings, Peter, weren't they?' said the policewoman.

Peter looked sideways at her.

'We've had experts look at those paintings. They

give her a mental age of about nine. I mean – her body had grown up but her mind didn't – couldn't grow up.' The policewoman watched him. 'She has the mind of a child, more or less. I'm sorry.'

Peter stared away from her. The policewoman began to bustle about with her papers. 'Cheer up! Did you know they've been seen? Oh, yes – you see it isn't all bad news.' She smiled again as he looked up hopefully. 'We found the man with the dog that bit her. He said she gave him the fright of his life – all dressed up in that blue thing.' She laughed. Peter smiled weakly. 'He said she looked like a Roman empress with it wrapped around her like a toga. And more important, some boys saw them the other day. That's right, they came across them lying among some bushes in Wolf's Wood, about fifty miles away.'

'And Amy's all right?' begged Peter.

'Amy's all right.' The policewoman frowned slightly. 'That's some giant, though. She did fifty miles in one night. Quite a feat.'

So they could be anywhere by now . . .

'Maybe she'll be back around here soon,' said Peter hopefully.

'Why do you think that?'

'Because the space ship's coming . . . I mean . . . she thinks the space ship's coming. Or do you think she was just lying?' he asked nervously.

'She thinks a space ship's coming for her? Yes, I see what you mean. I'll pass it on to the chief.'

She smiled and Peter smiled back. He would have

113

done anything to help catch her and get his sister back.

It was terrible and it was getting worse but she was so near, so near to getting home so she mustn't give up. There were only a few days to go. She was doing as she'd been told to do if ever she got lost, just as she had last time. It hadn't worked last time but she had to try again. She couldn't bear the thought of going back into the ground for another thousand years or more. She was weak now. If she had to do it again, she would never wake up.

The cold was bad. In the big dark building it had been cold at night but here in the outside the cold was far worse. The blue cloth was not much use. She was coughing, her lungs hurt. She wanted to run up and down but of course she couldn't. If they saw her they'd try to kill her, like last time.

The really big problem was food. So hungry! She'd eaten little enough in the cinema even though she was starving. The little one had brought so little – just a few apples and bread. After her long sleep recovering in the ground, waiting for the time to come, all she wanted to do was eat and eat and eat and eat and eat. But where was the food in this world? She'd gone out on her own at night and found food locked away in shop windows. She dared not break in for fear of getting caught.

And the little one, her friend. The giant had to help look after her. They had to help look after each other. The little one needed food and the giant

114

had no idea how to get it for her.

The problem was solved – so she thought – on the second night as they crossed a field. She was treading on hard, round things that crunched under her foot. By the starlight she could see them all around her – rows and rows of fat round plants in a little nest of leaves.

She bent to pull one up. She shook the soil off the roots and sniffed it.

It smelled good.

She bit into it. It was hard and crunchy and juicy and sweet. It filled her mouth with its juice and a wonderful, rich, tangy aroma filled her nostrils and mouth. It was good to chew, it was so crisp and solid. The giant stood in the field and crowed with excitement. She had discovered some wonderful exotic fruit. She offered one to her friend.

Amy tried to bite the cabbage like an apple the same as the giant did but of course it was too tough for her. She could hardly get her teeth around it. The giant sat down and smacked her lips; she obviously thought cabbages were delicious treats. She was gobbling them like strawberries. Amy watched her jealously and tried to nibble at the cabbage again, but it was cold and raw and tough.

'I don't like cabbage,' she said.

Poor Amy . . . she'd had nothing to eat for almost two days. Her stomach was so empty, it felt as if it was sucking at her ribs. Watching the giant eat she could almost feel the welcome food rushing into her stomach and around her blood. It was too much.

Amy burst suddenly into tears.

When the little one made that noise, Giant watched her in amazement, not recognising it for a moment. Her kind made a different noise when they cried. But the tears were the same. She touched the wet and understood. It was hunger, fear at being away from her parents, at being lost – at being with someone strange. All these things Giant knew herself. It would help if she had some food inside her.

Giant chewed up her cabbage, chewed and chewed until it was pulp. Then she took some out of her mouth and offered it.

Amy made a face and turned away. Disgusting . . . eating out of someone else's mouth! Giant was disappointed. She had nothing else to offer. She went back to her cabbage and wondered what to do.

Amy watched her. It was disgusting – but she was so terribly hungry. She leant up and reached up to Giant's mouth. Giant paused, opened her lips. Amy took a few shreds and quickly popped them in her mouth before she had a chance to think about it.

Funnily enough, once you did it, it wasn't bad. It didn't taste bad at all – not worse than cabbage did normally. Better even, because it was softer. She could eat it like this. Only you'd have to be as hungry as Amy was to want to.

The two sat in the field eating the cabbage – first the giant, then Amy from out of her mouth.

Towards dawn they came to the outskirts of a town. The sky was only just brightening at the edges but

116

people were up and about already. They could see the lights of cars running down the roads and moving in the town, and there were one or two buildings with the lights on.

Giant skirted around the town, Amy on her arm like a doll. It was time to find somewhere to hide.

Towns were good because they had deserted buildings but you had to get in when everything was very still and dark and there were no people up and about. But it was late. People were already up and about.

'We should find a barn or something,' said Amy. But Giant had other ideas. She moved closer to the houses. She found a field that led onto a street. She crossed a garden onto the road and began to creep up the street.

Amy could feel her shivering. It was partly the cold, partly fear. She was so much on her own, even with Amy there. She had no idea how to tell a used building from an unused one. She just had to hope Amy would spot one.

She was in luck.

'There!' Amy pointed. An ugly square building with lots of windows. The windows on the lower floor were blocked off. Many higher up were smashed.

It was getting quite light now. They could so easily be seen. Giant quickly ran round to the back of the factory and began to climb. She was a wonderful climber, despite her size. Her fingers and toes seemed to stick to the brickwork. Soon she was up

117

by the windows on the first floor. She found a smashed window and swung herself in.

Everything was bare and cold inside. She found the stairs and went down to where the windows were boarded to hide in the dark. She was a creature of the light, but darkness was one of her few friends in this place. She sat in a corner. She laid Amy down in the folds of her gown by her side. Amy sighed, cuddled up to her.

'Only a few days,' she said. 'Only a few days and you can go home.' Giant nodded and spread her long fingers to indicate joy.

Then they went to sleep.

The factory was a good place to hide. Boys sometimes broke in and wandered about at weekends but this was a weekday. No one came near. They both slept in the morning. In the afternoon, Amy woke up with stomach cramps. She was sick and then she had to go to the toilet over and over again.

'Those cabbages,' she groaned miserably. Giant was scared; her friend was sick. She had made her friend sick by feeding her cabbages. Or had she caught something from her mouth? Amy was her only friend; Amy had helped her. She would not let anyone harm Amy but how could she fight a bug like this?

The afternoon passed slowly. Amy threw up until her stomach was sore. She had to go to the toilet until it stung. She was hot. Giant got more and more nervous. She ought to make the little girl go home or leave her somewhere where she could get help. But the trouble with doing that was, she didn't believe she could survive undiscovered until next week if she had to do it on her own.

Amy tried to make her feel better. 'It's just a tummy bug,' she explained. 'I'll be all right in a bit.'

Giant was unsure. There was so little she could do to help her, to repay her for all she had done. But one thing she could do tonight – get Amy some proper food.

The darkness came slowly creeping over the town. First the cars put on their lamps, then the streets put on theirs. Still the town bustled and was full of people. It got quiet for a while but you could tell everyone was up because of the lights in the buildings. Only much later, well after dark, did the house lights go off one by one. Then there was another long wait until the night became really deep and still and there was no noise. Giant stretched her legs, put Amy on her arm and climbed down the side of the old factory to the ground. She waited a while in the shadows, making sure, watching. Then she slipped off along the quiet roads.

Amy sat on her arm. She felt so weak she barely noticed as Giant turned off into the town, not out of it. They were approaching some shops when she saw what was happening.

'What are you doing . . . where are you going?' she asked.

Giant turned to look at her. Her eyes sparkled.

It was an adventure. She was excited.

They were at a small supermarket. The lights were on low inside. They could see the food stacked in shelves, long, long shelves with every sort of food on them. Giant seized Amy's hand and pointed.

'Yes, but it's all locked up,' whined Amy. It was miserable looking at so much food without being able to get it. But Giant reached into her blue robe and pulled out a big stone. She tapped it lightly on the window.

Amy understood. The window could be broken. The food would be there for the taking.

'That would be stealing,' pointed out Amy. 'Anyway, you mustn't. You're so near to going home. You'll muck up everything.'

Giant shook her stone again. Amy glanced up and down the street and gave up. She needed that food. She pressed her nose to the window.

So much! Jam, milk, juice, cakes, biscuits . . . 'Chocolate biscuits!' hissed Amy excitedly. 'I want those – look!'

Giant looked. She frowned.

Amy sighed. How could she ever explain chocolate biscuits?

'All right then – over there . . .' She pointed to a great rack of bread, all in packets. Her stomach wanted something like that, stodgy and mild. Lots of it.

Giant nodded.

She took Amy and laid her down in the doorway. Amy sat and buried her head in her hands. She was terrified. 'You shouldn't,' she muttered. But she did want that bread.

Giant ran a few steps along the long window, away from Amy. She glanced up and down the street. She laid the stone on the window, lifted it back – and banged.

Nothing happened. The clear window just rocked under the blow. She banged again – again and again and still nothing happened. She was making a lot of noise. She was nervous of breaking the glass but now she was scared she would be heard. She took a step back, pulled back her hand and this time swung properly at it. The window shattered like water.

There was an enormous clash. It fell to the ground in shards and every shard crashed and clattered. Inside the store, a loud bell began to ring and there was a dog barking.

The glass was hanging in the window like terrible teeth. She pushed it in and it fell clattering to the floor. She climbed in carefully over the sharp teeth and ran to the bread. She seized a handful. From the back of the shop there was a shout. A door opened, there was a ferocious noise. Suddenly, around the corner of an aisle there was a big dog. It leapt up barking and growling when it saw her. It ran straight at her.

She screamed like a bird screaming. She'd known this before. It had all happened long ago.

The dog jumped at her. She swung her arm and it went flying in the air – over the cereal and the juice, falling heavily in the aisle on the other side. She ran for the window, but she slipped and fell onto the glass sticking up out of the frame. The savage glass teeth bit into her. She screamed again because the pain was terrible.

Amy appeared. The dog was coming back. Amy tried to help her up. She was bleeding heavily, groaning and weeping. She managed to stand up and get over the glass. Outside there were people gathered; they were standing ready to leap at her but they were scared. Giant put Amy on her arm and ran. Behind her the people were shouting in anger and surprise. Some began to give chase. A car started. Someone was driving after them.

Chapter 11

For a while the car was running side by side with them before Giant found a side alley where it couldn't follow. She ran quickly. Amy thought the wound must not be so bad after all – it had looked terrible, an open gash as long as Amy's arm in her side. Now they left the town; they were fleeing across the countryside in long smooth strides, eating up the miles, over fields, hedgerows, past villages and the streetlamps like necklaces of bright lights strung across the fields. Behind, their trail was left in splashes of red blood.

Amy had no idea where they were going. The country all looked the same to her in the dark. They ran for half an hour or more. At last Giant stopped. She groaned and held her side tightly but Amy saw the blood, black in the starlight, soaking through her gown.

'How bad is it?' she begged. Giant said nothing. She didn't need to. Amy, who shared her thoughts and feelings, could feel the remorse, the fear, the pain itself burning her up.

She put Amy down and clung to a tree and bent over, breathing hard. Amy staggered on her feet. She felt terrible herself. Her stomach hurt, she felt dizzy. There was a buzzing noise coming from inside her head. She looked round. They were by the river

123

in a pasture next to the hump of Barrow Hill. She could see the small trees in the distance, the great fallen oak lying dark in the water nearby.

'We're back home,' she said.

Giant looked at her. Home was a long, long way off – further than ever, now.

Slowly, Giant sat down on the fallen tree. She held her side. 'Let me see,' said Amy. She tenderly moved her arm to see the wound. The blue cloak was stained from her armpit to the hem in blood. Amy could see it dripping from the edge. Then she moved the cloak to see underneath, but she let it drop. The wound was too terrible to look at.

'We have to find a doctor.' Amy was filled with fear. Could it really end in death? She looked up at her big friend. 'Are you going to be all right?' she begged.

Giant didn't answer. She began to crawl forwards into the field. Amy followed, touching her shoulder, too small to help her in her last effort. She crawled forwards for five minutes on her hands and knees, too weak to stand anymore.

She managed to get back to the place. In a few nights the time would be right, the doorway would open – but too late for her. She had to go back into the dark, cold, wet earth to sleep, to heal – just as she had done last time when the people had chased her and shot her through with arrows, just as she had done the time before when she had first got lost.

Perhaps, in another five thousand years, she

would emerge and try again to be in the right place at the right time, but she doubted it. This was the third time she had had to hide in the earth and sleep. She was very weak. She had to try, but inside, Giant had little doubt that this time she would die under the ground.

She crawled until she found a young oak tree growing not far from Barrow Hill. Then she began to dig.

Amy watched as her friend tore handfuls of earth and stones out of the ground. She was burrowing, burrowing into the soil like a rabbit or a mole. It took a long time. The blood was still coming. At first it was easy but then the earth got thick and sticky and she slowed down. But slowly a hole formed, deep under the roots of the young oak.

It took over an hour, with many pauses to gather her strength. Amy tried to help, but there was no room for two working inside. The sun, a dangerous beacon in the sky, was rising as she worked. At the end Giant was barely moving. At last she lay still and rested. She was lying in the earth with her feet sticking out of the entrance.

Amy laid her hand on Giant's foot. She felt a soft tremor go through her. Heavily, slowly, Giant began to pull herself out and turn herself round. She wanted to lie with her face closest to the air. She wanted to say goodbye to Amy.

It took minutes but at last she lay as she wanted to, her feet curled up behind her, her face close to the entrance. Really the hole was not deep enough. Her face would only be a foot or so from the surface – not enough to hide her for ten years, let alone ten thousand.

Amy peered in at her. A pool of blood lay under her. The dawn was just beginning but she could see her eyes shining dully. Her face seemed to have changed colour.

She reached out for Amy, and the little girl came forward, half inside the hole, and put her arms around her.

'I'm sorry, I'm so sorry,' said Amy. She felt damp on her shoulder and looked up, thinking it was blood. But Giant was crying. She had lost her last chance of ever getting home. She was saying good-bye to everything.

They held each other for as long as they dared. But time was getting short. Weakly, Giant pushed Amy away. They watched each other for a moment. Then, she began to shovel the earth back in on herself. First her body, then her face disappeared under the earth. She looked a last time at Amy. Amy could see her eyes glinting. Then the big arm pulled in a final load of earth and it was still.

As Amy stood watching, the earth shook. Giant was shaking herself under the ground. The mound around her shook, and then suddenly fell in. The tree above her shook as if struck, then all was very still. Giant had collapsed the earth in on her tunnel and closed herself off.

Amy crept forward and began patting more earth

into place, patting it in to make the place as smooth as she could. The mud was cold and nasty. At the end she piled the turf back in its place.

It wasn't very good. There were gaps in between the turf. Anyone could see someone had been digging. Sooner or later, someone would get curious. A boy, a dog perhaps. As she stood up, Amy felt something stop inside her like a little death. The terrible fear and remorse that had been burning her up for the past hour had passed away. For the first time since the storm, she was truly on her own.

Giant was asleep – or dead. It was time to go home.

Amy walked across the field till she came to a road. She had a rotten headache, she was covered in sweat and she kept swaying on her feet, she felt so weak. All she wanted to do was lie down and rest, but she was too cold. She knew where she was but she kept walking away from home. She wanted to be as far away as possible so that if they began to look they wouldn't begin near to where Giant was hidden.

She was scared now that she was on her own – scared of the cars that drove past, scared of strangers. She hid in the hedges when anyone came. After a long time she came to a village. It was day by this time, everyone was up and about. She walked nervously down the main street. She felt as though she was looking out of a black pit which kept closing around the edges of her vision. She was covered in mud. People were staring at her. Then the stomach cramps started again and she retched and the people started to move towards her . . .

Chapter 12

Mornings were awful. During the day you could forget about it from time to time but in the morning it was there as soon as you woke. It stayed with you for ages.

They were at the breakfast table when the telephone call came. His grim mother went to answer it. They were all hoping, of course, but a telephone call could mean anything. Peter and his father ate their cereal and waited, listening for her voice . . .

'Oh, my God . . . she's safe, she's safe . . . Oh, thank God. Thank God . . . they've found her . . .'

And there was a wonderful explosion in his heart. He just sat and wept while his parents danced for joy around the table.

They went to the police station straight away but they left Peter behind. That wasn't fair. He could have done with that reunion – it was his fault, wasn't it? It was his reunion. But they went and he had to stay with a neighbour. Then, they came back without her. She was ill; she had to spend a couple of days in hospital for checks.

So then there were another couple of days when he wasn't allowed to see Amy. His parents saw her every day but they said they were worried he'd catch whatever it was she had. By the time she came back, it was all over and everyone was just being ordinary.

He stood in the hall and watched her coming in the front door. He felt awkward – as if he'd tried to murder her and she was coming to accuse him. But Amy, bless her, saw none of that. As soon as she saw him her whole face lit up, she ran to him and flung her arms around him.

'I missed you, I missed you,' she cried. Then she leaned close to him and whispered, 'You should have been with us . . .'

'Some virus or other, she'll soon be better,' the police doctor said easily. But there were other doctors – therapists, psychologists, analysts. The trouble was, Amy wasn't talking. No one could get anything out of her – where she'd been, who she'd been with, what had been said, what had happened to her.

The doctors believed something had happened to Amy so awful that she couldn't even think of it, let alone talk about it. She was pretending to herself and everyone else that it had never happened. Why else should she refuse to talk about those days when she had been away? They all questioned her – doctors, parents, police. Amy sat and stared straight ahead as if she had not heard.

'Do you want to help your sister?' the policewoman asked Peter, when she called to see him the same day Amy came home. Peter nodded. It was a stupid question – of course he wanted to help her.

'You can help by listening to her. Don't argue,'

she warned. 'Just talk to her about the woman, and about what happened. Don't press her, but if she does talk, listen carefully. Help her talk. She might tell you things she won't tell the grown-ups.'

Peter nodded his head, but he wasn't sure if he wanted to talk to Amy about that. So far she had said nothing, except that remark about how he should have been with them when she first came home. And if she did start to talk about it he wasn't sure how much he wanted to tell the policewoman. If she talked to him it meant she trusted him. At that time, it was important to Peter for someone to trust him.

Amy spent almost three days in bed. In the hospital she had been very ill indeed, but now the fever was down. She was still very weak. Her mother treated her as if she'd had an operation or something. Peter was allowed in every now and then, but he was always aware of his mother lurking at the door, making sure he didn't tire the invalid or say the wrong thing.

The journalists were still hanging about. They wanted the story, too. They wanted to buy it – they'd offered a lot of money. Peter heard his parents talking about it. It was so much money, it was almost enough to make them rich. But Amy wasn't talking and anyway, they weren't sure they wanted to sell.

One Saturday morning, five days after Amy had come home, their mother went out shopping and left the two children alone at home for the first time since Amy had disappeared. Peter was in his room playing with his cars, but he was thinking about his sister next door. He could hear her playing tapes on her cassette recorder. He could go through and try to talk to her now – about the giant, or just about anything. But he didn't want to.

He didn't dare.

He jumped when his door opened. She came in and kneeled down by him.

'I can't get out,' Amy said.

Peter looked at her sideways. He pushed his car along the carpet. 'You were naughty,' he told her. 'You're not to go out.' Then he added, 'That woman might be waiting for you again.'

It was the first time either of them had mentioned her. He felt her watching him.

There was a pause while she had a think. She said, 'You have to help me now.'

Peter stopped his game. He began to put his cars away. She was scaring him.

'You have to help me help her,' said Amy.

Peter sighed. 'Where is she?' he asked.

Amy looked carefully at him, deciding. At last she said, 'She went back into the ground.'

Peter felt a thrill of horror go through him. Back into the ground! What if she'd really buried herself? She'd be dead – in the ground!

Amy went on. 'She hurt herself. She fell on some glass and she was cut, she was bleeding everywhere. She was going to die. She had to go back into the ground to get better.'

132

Peter licked his lips. This was important. This was the sort of thing the policewoman wanted to know about, the sort of thing they were all waiting for – the doctors, the police, everyone. The mad woman had gone into the ground. They needed to know and he was finding out.

'Where is she in the ground?' he asked.

Amy looked at him closely but she didn't answer. 'Her people are coming,' she said.

Peter almost jumped. The space ship! He couldn't look at her. He could feel the hair bristling on his head. For the first time since the police had told him it was all just a story he realised that a part of him still believed every word Amy said. And he didn't want to.

Amy said, 'I knew you weren't really going to give her away, but she was scared, you see. I tried to tell her it was just you saying that but she didn't understand.'

Peter nodded. He felt terrible. What could he do? He took out his cars again. Amy frowned.

'Don't you understand?' she scolded. 'When her people come we have to meet them – to tell them where she is. They can rescue her.'

But Peter wouldn't meet her eye. 'She wasn't a giant,' he told her coldly. 'She was a mad woman – she was mad. You mustn't do anything like that again.'

Amy stared at him in horror. 'But you don't believe that – you don't!' she cried. 'You saw her!'

Peter was furious. She put her hands on his

133

shoulders but he shook her off. 'Go away!' he shouted suddenly. 'It was stupid, it was all stupid. Leave me alone.'

Amy's eyes filled with tears. Then they heard the latch on the front door go. Peter tried to speak, to say he was sorry or something, but she jumped up and ran away.

Peter went out that afternoon. He walked down to the river feeling wretched. He had no idea how to get out of this.

He wandered all around the fields, looking. It would be disturbed earth; it would be a grave. He wandered about for ages but he found nothing. At last he went back in. This evening, tomorrow . . . soon . . . he'd get in touch with the policewoman and tell her what Amy had said.

Later, he hung around in the living room watching telly. Amy avoided him. He wanted to talk to someone about it. He wanted to tell someone – Amy that he believed her, his parents that the mad woman was back in the ground – he didn't know what.

Tomorrow, he thought. Tomorrow, when he'd had a chance to find out more. Tomorrow he'd tell.

That evening, before bedtime, the wind began to blow.

It was dark. It was the middle of the night. He didn't know why he was awake. At first he thought it might be the wind that was raging across the roofs. Then he realised – someone was creeping across the floor towards him.

It was Amy, on all fours. She'd crept all the way from her bedroom like that, to be quiet. She leaned on his bed with her elbows.

She said, 'It's now.'

Peter stared at her face in fright. It was so dark he could barely make it out. It looked like a ghost's face. Outside the wind beat urgently on the windows.

'What?'

Amy nudged him. 'Come on . . .'

'How do you know?' he begged.

Amy shrugged. 'I just know,' she said. 'I knew I'd know,' she added proudly.

Peter thought of all the other things she'd known – what the woman wanted, what she felt, what she meant. Under the warm covers, Peter shivered.

Amy stood up by the bed. 'Get dressed,' she ordered.

Peter got out of bed. He had to talk to her, but not here so close to his parents. He didn't get dressed, he just pulled on his dressing-gown. Amy said, 'You'll be cold,' but he didn't reply.

He was certain his mother would wake up when they went downstairs – she slept so lightly these days. But they got down into the kitchen all right. Peter stood in the middle of the floor, listening to the wind across the meadows. Amy went to the drawers by the sink. She had a bag on her shoulder. She took the torch out of the drawer and put it in

135

her bag. Then she went to the door.

It was locked.

Thank heaven it was locked! Of course his parents had made sure there would be no more midnight wanderings. Now they couldn't get out and he didn't have to say no.

'Where's the key?' she asked.

'I don't know.' That was a lie. It was hidden on top of a kitchen cupboard.

Amy was getting panicky. 'We have to get out, Peter. We have to tell them where to find her or she'll die . . .'

Peter stood still and watched.

'The window! Peter, the window . . .'

Peter looked up. The tall window looking out over the back garden . . . There was just a catch – that was easy, but then there was the lock at the top. The key was always left on the window-sill under a mat. Already Amy had it and was climbing up. How could his father and mother be so stupid as to leave the key there!

Amy reached up – but she was too short. Only Peter was tall enough to reach the lock.

'Peter – please, Peter . . .'

Peter stood still.

'Peter . . .!' She was shocked, shocked. He was betraying her.

And then there came the footsteps along the landing. His father, long and slow steps. They held their breaths. The toilet door opened. They heard him peeing. When he came out he'd look in their rooms. They always looked these days, every time, every night. Peter had woken up and heard them, felt them peeking in on him and Amy to make sure she was safe and he was there.

The toilet flushed.

'Peter, she'll die. Peter, please . . .!'

Amy was crying. She was crying because she had no doubt, because she knew. Peter glanced at her, upstairs, at his hands that had to do something.

Amy knew. She always had known.

And in that second, so did he. It was only for a minute, but he believed. They were all wrong, the ones who should know best – the police, his parents, the doctors. They didn't know. Amy knew. He believed just long enough to jump up onto the window-sill and snatch the key and put it in the lock. He believed long enough to open the window and watch Amy jump down. He pulled the curtain behind him so his parents wouldn't see at first.

Peter jumped down into the windy garden.

Hand in hand, they ran across the lawn. The wind was so strong in their backs they flew like scraps of paper. By the time they reached the stile into the field, Peter had already begun to doubt. The woman was waiting for them, it would be death this time. But it was too late.

At the fence they heard a shout, a scream of fear and anger. Peter's bedroom light was on. His father had found the empty beds. They climbed the stile and blew in the dark across the fields towards the river. The grass writhed in the meadows around

137

them as they ran. They couldn't use the torch or they'd be spotted. They tripped and fell, got up and ran and tripped and fell ... They had to stop soon because they had no breath. Amy was gasping – she'd been ill, she was weak. Peter was chilled and his heart was beating madly.

He was so scared! He'd been stupid again – hadn't he?

'Is she out here?' he begged. He had to shout because the wind was so big, rushing in the grass all around them. 'Tell me . . .' Was it a trick to get him to the mad woman because she wanted to get him?

'I told you, she's in the ground,' said Amy angrily. He should believe her! 'They're coming to get her.'

Peter seized her arm.

'Is there a space ship?' he begged. He'd give anything to see a space ship.

Amy frowned. 'Something . . . I don't really know,' she said.

There was a tearing noise around them. The trees were coming down again.

Amy led him, running across the bumpy pasture. There was so little time, and they had to fight every inch of the way with the wind. But as they ran . . . the wind stopped. It just seemed to die. One minute everything was flapping and wailing, the next . . . the night was still. The two children stopped running and stared at each other in a thrill.

'Where are we going?' whispered Peter.

'To Barrow Hill. But . . .' In the darkness it was

138

all strange. The fact was, with no Giant to lead her, Amy had got lost.

Peter looked around. Where were the landmarks? Here was the river, there were the rushes and the tall poplar tree, dying with its roots in the water . . .

'This way . . .'

They were near, but it was so dark. He almost thought he was lost too, but then the moon came out and they saw it, the old hill – the grass on its slopes silvery in the light of the moon.

There was nothing else to be seen.

Amy's voice was near to tears. 'I thought . . .'

'What?'

'It should be here now . . .'

Peter stared at the empty hill. His face felt cold, he felt Amy's hand cold in his. She was wrong. She had always been right but now she was wrong. And the police would be coming. His parents would have rung them up. They would be coming now, searching the fields in long rows with lights and dogs . . .

And the mad woman was out here with them.

Peter felt sick. He'd done it again . . .

'Amy,' he said. 'Amy, we have to go home now.'

Amy was staring at the hill as if she could make the ship appear.

'We'd better go back,' said Peter. He was trying to sound normal, as if everything was all right. That was their only hope – to get back at once before she found them.

'Amy . . .'

'They're coming, they're coming . . .!' she hissed. She shook his hand off again and stared fiercely ahead, waiting.

Amy cried, 'Look at the moon!'

Peter looked up. The familiar white face stared down at him, smudged by dust and cloud.

'Not that one – over there!'

Peter turned and followed her finger. A second moon hung over Barrow Hill.

It was no moon of the earth. Round and full tonight, it was larger than our moon. It was yellow and orange and blue. It was shining with the light from another sun.

Two moons. Two skies. Two worlds. They travelled the great deserts between the stars not in a machine, but by twisting space and time in a great loop, once in every five thousand of our years. Tonight, our world and their world existed side by side. The moon that Peter and Amy saw was not really a moon; it was Giant's home planet. But they still needed a machine to travel the distance through space that was left between their world and ours, and now the children saw that, too.

At first it was as if the clouds and stars and the moonlight on the barrow were disappearing. Then there was – something. It began to show itself with the kind of light when something very pale is sitting in the darkness – with a kind of dull shine. It was so huge! At first they thought it was as big as the barrow. Then they saw that it *was* the barrow. The grass and round earth was disappearing and in its place came the tall loops, the long runners and long, curved body, towering over the children, over the fields, blotting out the sky and stars. Perhaps, on the other planet shining on this strange night in the sky, the hill with its grassy flanks was appearing in the place of the ship, in this very same way.

A doorway opened. They came out.

There were two of them, a man and a woman. At first they looked small in comparison to the space ship. As they got closer, they looked suddenly huge. They were the same as the giant – the same tall, graceful form and long, still faces, the same terrible, quivering snout. But they were as tall as her again.

'But they're so big,' said Peter.

'Didn't you know?' scoffed Amy.

He was about to say, 'Know what?' but as he opened his mouth he realised what she was telling him. Giant was a child – a child no older than she was.

The two people stood about seven metres tall. They looked down, the children looked up. It was very tense but very quiet. They didn't need to talk. They had other ways of understanding each other, and Amy shared them. They knew by being with her, by her being there, just as she knew by being with her friend. Peter glanced at her. Her face shone. She'd had a terribly difficult task and she'd done it for her friend. Now she ran suddenly forward. Peter was astonished at her bravery, but of course she could understand these people in ways he could not. She grabbed the tall man by the leg, pointed down to the tree where her friend was buried and yelled – not to say anything to him, just to make the thought in her mind the stronger. The tall man followed her finger, and ran down the hill to the place in the bank where she pointed. He got to his knees and began to claw the loose earth away in great handfuls.

Amy stood at the feet of the tall woman. She stared up at her for a moment, took a step forward. The giant woman opened her arms and Amy ran to her and then screamed in delight as she was rushed twenty feet into the air. The giant cradled her next to her cheek and kissed her. Amy hugged her back. She knew at once that this woman and her friend were somehow part of each other – mother and child, sisters, friends, she didn't know what. She did know that they both loved the injured girl now being exposed in the hillside.

Below, the other giant dug. It did not take long; Giant had had the strength to only just cover herself with soil. Soon the ragged hair was showing, like a cluster of roots. When Amy saw her friend's head exposed in the soil she screamed to be put down and ran forward to hold her.

All this time, Peter had been standing to one side, not knowing what to do. He had no understanding as Amy had. He was scared, lost, apart from them. But now the big woman took a couple of steps towards him. Instinctively he raised his hand as if to shield her off and turned his head away. But her hands as they closed about him were gentle. She picked him up as if he were a shrew or a mouse – some small animal that might even so have a nasty bite. She laid him for a second to her cheek and he put out his arms and embraced her big head. He wanted to say that he was sorry he had got it so wrong, that he wasn't like Amy who knew things somehow – but he'd got it right at the end, after all.

Then she turned and put him down next to the still form of Giant and bent down to see if the child was all right.

Amy laid her hands on the still, cold face, stained with clay. The mud underneath Giant was clotted with dark blood. She was cold, not breathing. The man placed his hands on her and stroked warmth back into her blood. There was a long slow moment when it was only blood and pain, but at last the long eyelashes trembled, fluttered, and opened.

'See? I told you it would be all right!' cried Amy crossly. She buried her head in Giant's neck and hugged her and hugged her. Her friend gazed around her at the sight she thought she'd lost forever. She was terribly ill. But before her people took her back she managed to raise her hand to her mouth and make one last smile for Amy.

An Angel for May

Melvin Burgess

Tam often takes refuge in the ruins of Thowt It
Farm when he is unhappy at home. One day he
follows an old beggar woman and her dog to
the farm and is transported back to the Second
World War. There he makes friends with May,
who has been rescued from a bombed-out
house and now refuses to eat or sleep indoors.
When Tam gets into trouble in the town, May
comes to his rescue. She tries to persuade him
to stay at Thowt It, but Tam is afraid of being
permanently trapped in the past.

'An atmospheric, eerie book ... it handles a
time slip in a completely believable way'
– Carnegie Medal judges

Shortlisted for the Carnegie Medal

The Baby and Fly Pie

Melvin Burgess

We're the rubbish kids, losers and orphans. Every day we go out on to the Tip to sort rubbish for Mother Shelly.

For Sham, Fly Pie and his sister Jane, this is the grim reality of their lives. Then one day everything changes when they find a baby on the Tip – a baby worth seventeen million pounds.

The events that follow take them into a savage, lonley city and so begins an endless fight for survival.

'… totally gripping and charged with intense emotion' – *Mail on Sunday*

'Gritty and realistic, this novel touches and challenges, and certainly can't be put down' – *Books for Keeps*

Shortlisted for the Carnegie Medal

Pongwiffy

Kaye Umansky

Pongwiffy is a very smelly witch of very dirty habits. But she is a happy witch – until a gruesome gang of goblins move in next door and make her life miserable. So she asks her not-so-best friend Sharkadder to help her find a new slum and to advertise for a much-needed familiar. The trouble is, the only reply Pongwiffy gets is from a hamster! How will she explain this to the Witches' Covern?

Pongwiffy and the Goblins' Revenge

Kaye Umansky

Pongwiffy's broomstick (Woody) is out of control! He refuses to obey orders, he won't stand still – and whenever goblins are mentioned he faints! Pongwiffy is at her wits' end. But doesn't know that worse is still to come – the wicked Goblins are hatching a dastardly plot. Only Woody knows the dreadful secret. Will he be able to make Pongwiffy understand in time?

Pongwiffy and the Holiday of Doom

Kaye Umansky

Pongwiffy is depressed. It is raining in
Witchway Wood. Her fire has gone out and she
hasn't been invited to tea for ages. Pongwiffy
needs some excitement! So when a holiday
brochure plops on to the doormat, she springs
into action. Soon Brooms, Familiars and
Witches are off to the seaside for a holiday they

Pongwiffy and the Spell of the Year

Kaye Umansky

Pongwiffy is over the moon when she finds
Granny Malodour's famous Wishing Water
recipe. She is certain it will be the winning
entry for the Spell of the Year Competition. But
getting hold of the very unusual ingredients is
not an easy task and it lands Pongwiffy in big
trouble!

Pongwiffy and the Pantomime

Kaye Umansky

Pongwiffy is certain a pantomime is just the
thing to liven up Witchway Wood. She even
says she will write it! With a little help, the
panto is soon written. But then disaster strikes:
the pantomime horse is stolen from under the
Witches' noses by their arch-rivals the Goblins!

The Cay

Theodore Taylor

Adrift on the ocean, then marooned on a tiny
deserted island, a young boy and an old man
struggle for survival.

This is as intense and compulsive as only a
survival story can be; it is also a fascinating
study of the relationship between Phillip, white,
American, and influenced by his mother's
prejudices, and the black man upon whom
Phillip's life depends.

Timothy
of the Cay

Theodore Taylor

RESCUED: 12-YEAR-OLD BOY PHILLIP
ENRIGHT AND HIS CAT FROM
UNCHARTED CAY

Phillip has survived, despite being blind, for
four months on a tiny, remote, desert island.
But although Timothy, the old black sailor who
saved him from drowning, died before his
rescue, his wisdom and spirit continue to
inspire Phillip to risk an operation which might
restore his sight and enable him to return to the
cay to see it for the first time.

In this compelling story, Phillip's ordeal is
dramatically set along side a moving account of
Timothy's long struggle to realize his dream of
being captain of his own ship.

A powerful, wonderfully inspiring book.

Buster and the Black Hole

Betsy Duffey

Buster Jones, author, feels as if he's in a black hole.

He's had to give up his room to his grandfather. He's had to give up his beloved typewriter to his horrible sister. His mother is in a state, his father is hardly there and – worst of all – he's got writer's block.

Will he ever finish his new book, *Space Cows*? And how is he going to write a brilliant, moving speech about pickles?

The Weekly Ghost

Toby Forward

When Stephanie and her friends start The
Weekly Post, they are astonished to find that a
front page story in the first edition has been
changed overnight to a shocking new story.
Even more strangely, the paper's name has
been changed to The Weekly Ghost. Who has
been tampering with their newspaper?

READ MORE IN PUFFIN

For children of all ages, Puffin represents quality and variety – the very best in publishing today around the world.

For complete information about books available from Puffin – and Penguin – and how to order them, contact us at the appropriate address below. Please note that for copyright reasons the selection of books varies from country to country.

On the worldwide web: www.puffin.co.uk

In the United Kingdom: Please write to *Dept. EP, Penguin Books Ltd, Bath Road, Harmondsworth, West Drayton, Middlesex UB7 0DA*

In the United States: Please write to *Consumer Sales, Penguin USA, P.O. Box 999, Dept. 17109, Bergenfield, New Jersey 07621-0120*. VISA and MasterCard holders call 1-800-253-6476 to order Penguin titles

In Canada: Please write to *Penguin Books Canada Ltd, 10 Alcorn Avenue, Suite 300, Toronto, Ontario M4V 3B2*

In Australia: Please write to *Penguin Books Australia Ltd, P.O. Box 257, Ringwood, Victoria 3134*

In New Zealand: Please write to *Penguin Books (NZ) Ltd, Private Bag 102902, North Shore Mail Centre, Auckland 10*

In India: Please write to *Penguin Books India Pvt Ltd, 706 Eros Apartments, 56 Nehru Place, New Delhi 110 019*

In the Netherlands: Please write to *Penguin Books Netherlands bv, Postbus 3507, NL-1001 AH Amsterdam*

In Germany: Please write to *Penguin Books Deutschland GmbH, Metzlerstrasse 26, 60594 Frankfurt am Main*

In Spain: Please write to *Penguin Books S. A., Bravo Murillo 19, 1° B, 28015 Madrid*

In Italy: Please write to *Penguin Italia s.r.l., Via Felice Casati 20, I–20124 Milano*

In France: Please write to *Penguin France S. A., 17 rue Lejeune, F–31000 Toulouse*

In Japan: Please write to *Penguin Books Japan, Ishikiribashi Building, 2–5–4, Suido, Bunkyo-ku, Tokyo 112*

In South Africa: Please write to *Longman Penguin Southern Africa (Pty) Ltd, Private Bag X08, Bertsham 2013*